XO

Ashley
Bostock

TEMPTATION DEEP

ASHLEY BOSTOCK

Jordyn
Not sure this book would be what it is without your help.

ALL THE THINGS

1

QUINN

"You're such a brownnoser." Elizabeth scoffed at me while I tried to hook my laptop to our living room TV. "A brownnoser in cute shorts. My shorts that you borrowed and never returned."

"I am not a brownnoser. This is Dad's birthday. It's special to him. Mom's no longer here to spoil him. I try to do something every year for him. I don't want him to be sad and lonely every birthday without Mom. I want him to know how important he is and how much I appreciate him."

The thumbnail for the video popped up on the television. *Success.* I ignored her about the shorts because I looked great in them and wasn't returning them. "Besides, I can't help it if I'm the good daughter."

Elizabeth rolled her eyes. "How long did it take you to find all these pictures?"

Between work and my last week of volunteering for Habitat for Humanity, rounding up a hundred or so pictures of my parents and us girls had taken a week longer than I'd wanted. I'd stayed up until three this morning making sure the images were in perfect sync with the music. "It took me about three weeks to comb through everything without him finding out what I was doing. Which was no easy feat since we both work during the day." I looked around for my dad but didn't see him. "And mostly, all of the pictures were up here." I pointed under the TV where my mom had kept all of her photo albums.

"I'll go find Dad. I have to go soon."

Figures. Elizabeth had never enjoyed hanging out at our dad's social events. With Elizabeth gone and everyone else in the room in conversation, I pulled out my phone.

"Quinn, so lovely to see you." Kimber Emery gave me a large smile. "Your father mentioned you take the bar exam soon. Congratulations." It was weird seeing one of my old professors standing next to me in my own living room. "He's pretty proud of you," she said.

"Thank you." I tucked my phone into the waistband of my shorts. "Yeah, I can take it in July. He's told anyone who will listen how proud he is."

We both glanced into the kitchen, where my dad was talking to some of the other partygoers. Elizabeth tapped his shoulder and pointed to my setup. My dad had "business parties" at least once a month. But tonight, he was forty-eight, and apparently, that was still considered "a pup" to some of his friends. But I think my dad was feeling the effects of turning another year older—closer to fifty. His mind felt like he was thirty, but his body didn't. Those were his words.

"I just hope I'll pass on the first try so I don't have to wait until February to take it again."

Dad moved away from his friends, with Elizabeth trailing behind him. He wrapped his arm around me. "This one is growing up. Catching up to me in age."

I rolled my eyes. "Dad, I'm twenty-five. Almost twenty-six. I'm not even close to catching up to you."

He squeezed my nose.

Kimber gave me a dazzling smile that made me feel inadequate in the looks department. She was drop-dead beautiful in her four-inch cream-colored heels and flowered summer dress. Her perfect cherry-painted lips surely made other women envious, including me. "You were always a great student. I'm sure you'll be fine."

I put on my best polite smile, hoping she would find another person to have a conversation with. It wasn't like I hated her. I just didn't want to hang out with one of my old professors on a Friday night at my house. "Thank you." I nodded to my laptop. "It's time."

Elizabeth rounded up his guests, and I started the slideshow. Even though I'd watched it a million times, it still made me weepy. My dad when he was a little boy. Him and my mom at their high school prom. Their graduation. Them baptizing Elizabeth, standing outside of our church with Jason and Holly. The photos floated by, and I glanced at my dad. His eyes were watery, but he had the biggest grin on his face. Just what I'd wanted—to see him truly happy.

The slideshow ended, and he slung his arm over my shoulder. "Thanks, Quinn. How did you do that? Where'd you find all of those pictures?"

I leaned into him. "Around the house. I had to be sneaky so you wouldn't find out." I smiled at him. "I wanted to do something special for you. Happy birthday."

He kissed my forehead. "Happy day, indeed."

"I wish Mom was here." I blinked, not wanting tears to fall.

"Me too."

"I have to go, guys. Dad, love you. Quinn, see you later."

Elizabeth was already on her phone as she walked out the front door.

My dad got lost in the crowd, and I unplugged my laptop and turned off the computer before putting his music back on low. I reached for my laptop and glanced up to find Kimber approaching Jason Richter. I stopped. A big smile graced Jason's face. The smile was real because his dimples showed.

Jason and Kimber? I stood taller, straining to hear their conversation.

Jason didn't date anyone. Ever. As far as I knew, after Holly divorced him, no woman had been able to steal his attention. I'd seen plenty of women hit on him. In fact, anywhere we went in public, women came up to him, and he was always cordial, but he *never* brought women to events with him. Not like my dad's other single friends.

He was untouchable in that aspect. At least I'd thought he was, until now. He and Kimber, with their heads together, looked as if they were having a little more than just a friendly chit-chat. I couldn't hear what they were talking about because of the low rock music filtering out of the sound system.

Damn it, why did I turn that back on?

I watched their interaction. His eyes traveled up and down her body. Her hand went out and grazed his arm. Something tugged against my heart. Why was I watching them? Why did I *care?*

Jason had been one of my dad's best friends for as long as I remembered. Every time I saw him, I was transported back to age seven and our old house with the glitter in the ceiling where Jason twirled me around and around while Joan Jett rocked about how much she loved rock and roll. I laughed, thinking about the time I'd cooked him and Holly and my parents dinner on my parent's anniversary when I was fourteen. The good times. When my mom was still around. Before Holly divorced Jason. When we were all one big happy family.

I studied Jason a little more closely. He had aged *so* well. His hair was light brown with a neat trim against his neck. A thin white line at the hairline, where his skin hadn't seen the sun quite as much as the rest of his tanned body had, indicated he'd had it cut recently. Jason's dimples were so prominent, like usual. It was weird how he looked the same to me as he had all my life, but viewing him through Kimber's eyes, Jason was one sexy motherfucker. He was a lawyer, so naturally, he was sporting a white button-down shirt with the sleeves rolled up. His forearms were all muscle, and I knew the rest of him was too.

Does Kimber? For an older man... why am I thinking about him like this? I'd never taken much time to appreciate his looks before. And why would I? He was like a comfortable leather chair I saw nearly every day—always reliable and taken for granted.

There must have been some cosmic force in the air because Jason's eyes connected with mine, even as he spoke to Kimber. The look in his eyes was saying, "*Fuck me, beautiful,*" which was undoubtedly meant for Kimber. But it didn't stop the short bursts of desire against my clit—*What the actual hell?*

Oh my god. If any man in this group of stuffy doctors, lawyers, and dentists could bring me pleasure, it would be Jason.

He gave me a single nod, eyeing me like he could read my dirty thoughts, and I swallowed. It would absolutely be him.

Embarrassed that I'd been caught watching them, I

looked away, and my gaze landed on my neighbor, Dustin. He was also a good friend of my dad's. Dustin had to be almost fifty, as well. The three of them had gone to college together for the first four years and been in the same fraternity. It was purely coincidental that Dustin had moved in next door to us. Like I was holding some magic wand, Dustin met my gaze from across the room.

He tilted his tumbler in my direction, and it warmed me that he'd acknowledged me, which was crazy because he used to give me piggyback rides when I was younger. His girlfriend glanced over at me and gave me a small smile, but since she was only a two-weeker, she quickly went back to her task at hand—Dustin.

Don't blame you, Sheila.

Something must have been in the air. What was it about Dustin and Jason that was attracting my attention for the first time in my life?

My phone vibrated with another text from Jessie. *I just danced with this guy! Eeeee. I think we're going to the bar.*

I rolled my eyes. It was probably because Jessie kept texting me pictures of all these cute guys. I texted back. *Could you stop?!*

What would she think if I sent her a picture of Jason and Dustin? She might think it was gross that I was checking out men who were my dad's age. I darkened my screen, ignoring her for now.

I said hi to a few more partygoers—one was a lawyer who had such a conservative disposition I couldn't help but think I would have to shake stuff up a bit when I got my license to practice. *Couldn't they be a little more free-spirited sometimes?* Thankfully, Jason and Kimber were no longer in the living room, so I didn't have to experience those inappropriate feelings again.

I made my way to the hall to reach the stairs to my room and met my dad coming out of the bathroom. "Bed, Quinn?"

I glanced at my phone. "It's only nine."

"Figured you're bored to death. Not to mention tired from all the canning you did today. The jam looks great. I can't wait to have some in the morning."

"Thanks. The strawberries were perfect. It came out pretty good." I turned back to the kitchen. "I could start drinking with you guys." I generally tried not to have *too* much fun around my dad. Plus, I'd already had a cucumber martini earlier when my dad was opening his couple of gifts, and that had given me a small buzz.

"Ha, ha. Hit the road, kid."

"I'll be hanging out in my room. Ready to party when you guys are all ready for bed," I teased. But really, I was tired, and I rarely stayed up late. Plus, I only had a few pages left of *Dead Man's Folly*. I could finish reading it and go to bed.

My dad let out a full belly laugh, and I laughed with him. He was having a great time, and I was happy for him. He deserved to be happy after everything he had gone through.

The third step down creaked, and I almost slipped on the last step. *Am I buzzed?* I shook my head. It wasn't fuzzy in the least. I hadn't completely packed up my old room, but I'd already moved all my clothes and bedding into the basement. It was a master suite with a large walk-in closet and a bathroom bigger than my old room. It was heaven. The only thing I didn't care for was that the bathroom had a second door that led to the rec room, so anytime the party moved downstairs, I had to shut my door and share *my* bathroom, where the proper amount of illumination told me that I had left the light above the shower on.

I was surprised the party hadn't moved down there yet tonight. Although it wasn't playing any CDs, my dad's jukebox was lit up, and the light above the pool table cast a bright circle over the purple velvet, enticing anyone to play.

Finally in my own space, I pulled off my tank top as I entered my room, ready for something more comfortable. I reached for the light switch. Unmistakable moans and groans pulled my gaze to the bathroom.

Shit. Who in the hell is fucking in my bathroom? Why didn't they at least shut the door all the way?

I took a few steps closer, holding my crumpled tank top to my bra. The light from the pool table shone through the other side of the doorway. Even though it was partway shut, ample light filled the bathroom.

I held in my gasp. My hand instinctively covered my mouth. My stomach bottomed out like I'd gone over the hill of a roller coaster. Jason—hot Jason with his shirt sleeves rolled up, exposing his forearms. The same guy who I imagined eye-fucked me less than twenty minutes ago in my living room leaned against my bathroom counter, all sexy swagger. His one hand gripped the ledge of the marble, his strong thighs were spread out a little bit, and his jeans were still mostly on—only exposing his massive cock and the skin along his hips and part of his ass.

Holy, holy, holy. For the love of all that's holy, am I seeing things right? Am I drunk? Sleeping? I blinked, hoping it would make things clearer. *Did I fall down the stairs and hit my head? Am I really lying in a hospital bed, hallucinating?*

I blinked again, but the devastatingly beautiful scene in front of me was still there.

What am I looking at?

I couldn't tear my gaze away. I sucked in a breath. It was better than any filthy porn I'd ever watched, so painstakingly provocative that my clit was quivering with need.

He was fucking Kimber's mouth. She took him in her mouth so expertly, in and out. Her red lips fit around him magnificently—like they were meant for him. She pulled back on a pop, and a string of saliva caught between the head of his cock and her cherry lips.

Fuck me.

It was raw beauty. For a split second, it was me kneeling there, and I grew wetter. He was beautiful down there. Solid and large. Perfection. Even with his cock covered in saliva from another woman's mouth, Jason Richter was irresistible.

Should I be ashamed of watching my father's best friend get head? No fucking way.

Jason's hand was on Kimber's head. He watched her lick him like a lollipop. When she took him all the way in her mouth, he let out a groan. Her lips touched his pelvis. *Deep.*

"Fuck yes," he groaned in this husky voice I'd never heard before. Tingles floated from my nipples to my toes. He was beautiful everywhere. The way he stood. His sinful voice. Even the way he moved was beautiful.

I appreciated how he wasn't coming in her mouth right away. Giving my ex-boyfriend a blow job usually lasted for two minutes, if that. But not Jason. Kimber had folded up a towel and was using it to cushion her knees—like she'd known she would be down there for a while. Some women had all the luck.

I'd had no idea they were a couple. *Explains the flirting.* I'd also had no idea watching something like this in person would affect me so deeply. My toe nudged my tank top on the carpet. *When did I drop that?* I was a deer in the headlights, standing there in my bra and shorts, unable to look away.

Jason was in his element. His hips thrust in time to Kimber's mouth as she took him in and out. I was in awe at how they worked together in perfect harmony—he would thrust in, then she would pull back. In and out. His mouth was partway open in bliss.

I couldn't stop myself from putting pressure on my clit with my free hand. I was dying. I was totally fucking my dildo tonight when this episode was over. Maybe even getting out my wand.

Jason bit down on his bottom lip and wrapped her hair around his fist. His thrusts started increasing in speed. My nipples zinged with electricity. *Definitely getting out my wand. Most definitely.* Was he going to come inside her mouth? Pull out? I didn't even care. I wanted to see his beautiful face when he came. The nerves in my clit pulsed wildly—much more wildly than I've ever experienced in my life.

Jason grunted again, low and long, like a lion purring from his throat, making my own chest vibrate. "I'm going to come," he said, in a voice equally low and seductive as fuck.

My phone lit up with a text message, illuminating me in the darkness of my room. *Fuck.* I didn't look at it. I couldn't miss Jason getting off. But there was no question that I was busted. I made no attempt to move. This was the dirtiest moment in my life. Jason's gaze penetrated my soul, and I imagined he was telling me all sorts of filthy things with those beautiful eyes. His lips went into a smirk before he muttered, "Fuck," in the sexiest voice I'd ever heard.

His deft hips flexed forward while he held Kimber's head still, and he filled her mouth with his glorious come, all the while, never taking his eyes off mine.

2

JASON

I gripped the steering wheel as I turned onto Park Avenue then crept down the familiar street at a slower pace than usual. When Greg texted me about tonight's party, I'd considered cancelling. After Quinn caught me getting my dick sucked off in their basement last month, I couldn't say I was thrilled to show my face there. I'd talked to Greg a few times by text since then, and he sounded the same, so I could only imagine Quinn hadn't mentioned anything to him.

I had replayed that moment over and over in my head a million times, even when I knew better not to. *But fuck...*

What had Quinn been doing down there? Kimber and I had snuck down to the basement because Quinn's room was on the main floor, and since the party hadn't moved to the basement, it was either there or outside.

Quinn, half naked, and Kimber's mouth on me... I'd been too far gone to stop. She had stood there so enthralled by watching us, with her perky little tits—and it'd made me explode even quicker. I'd sworn she was touching her fucking pussy. But it'd all happened so fast, I wasn't sure.

It was that moment that I'd noticed she'd really grown up and turned into a woman. I pretty much squelched those thoughts anytime they came into my head. I was a creep for even thinking about her in that bra or how my cock would look against her lips.

I squeezed my eyes shut, trying to block the image. I was a perv.

But the interest from Quinn? I was fucking forty-six, but I knew when there was interest. I'd never in a million years even thought about her being attracted to me. *Or watching me come inside Kimber's mouth? Shit.* I adjusted my dick in my jeans, wondering how wet Quinn had gotten while watching us. Was she supremely innocent? Experienced? No way, as beautiful as she was, could she still be a virgin. Most annoyingly, the one thought I kept circling back to over and over was whether *she* gave head.

Fuck. I gripped my steering wheel tighter. I had no business having those thoughts about my best friend's daughter. It was wrong on so many levels.

By luck, there was an empty spot in their driveway, and I pulled my Lexus into it. The house lights were blazing, couples were streaming in and out, and my heart rate sped up at the thought of Quinn being inside.

Maybe I would be fortunate enough that she wasn't there. Would she be totally disgusted having to face me? After that episode, I'd pulled Kimber up and safely guided her out of the bathroom so that she'd never know we'd had eyes on us. She would have been embarrassed as hell.

But not me. No. I'd been fucking turned on. Pathetic.

If Kimber didn't show up tonight, it wouldn't be all bad. We'd gone out a few times before the head incident and had actually slept together since the first date. Professor Kimber was a wild one, despite her rigid syllabus and iron fist in class. I didn't want more than our casual dating, but Kimber did. I wasn't ready for that.

I opened the car door and stepped out. *Showtime.*

I scanned the street and the few cars I could see parked outside Greg's. At first glance, I didn't see Kimber's mini-van, and that was a plus. I pretended that I wasn't even looking for Quinn's white soft-top Jeep—which I didn't see.

The front door was open, so I walked in carrying my six-pack and held open the door for a guy I didn't know. "How's it going?"

"Ah. Good. I'm Kevin Lenard. Commercial real estate." He put out his right hand, and I gave it a solid shake.

"I'm Jason Richter. Of Richter, Richter & Salazar. I specialize in real estate legal matters." I nodded for Kevin to go in ahead of me. I'd walked in this house a million times over the years; it was practically my own. "How do you know Greg?"

Kevin nodded. "I met Greg through my brother. We hit it off pretty good, and he told me about the monthly get-togethers."

"Well, come on in. Lots of people to meet."

Greg was one of three guys who set up these monthly parties. The original plan had come from getting with other business professionals and talking about work. The problem was that by the time the second Saturday of the month rolled around, everyone wanted to kick back and drink more than they wanted to talk about work.

The Brenning house sparkled like it usually did, thanks to the house cleaning crew Quinn had hired when Debra was sick. And even though Quinn had moved back into the house to help take care of Debra, neither of them had known how to use a mop, so the cleaning crew had stuck around.

Oh shit. And there was Quinn.

I swallowed. My eyes were already taking in her long legs and supple skin. I closed my eyes for a second. Two minutes in, and I was having crazy creeper thoughts about my best friend's youngest daughter.

My eyes went to the photo of Debra, Greg, and the girls. The portrait was at least ten years old, when Debra had still looked healthy, before the cancer had started eating her away.

Crazy how times have changed.

Quinn was coming out of the kitchen with her friend Hannah. She hadn't noticed me, and I was too busy trying *not* to be noticed by her, that I looked away.

Thankfully, the new guy nudged my arm. "Mind if I hang with you until I see Greg?"

I nodded. Rock music was coming from the sound system in the living room. A few of the regular couples who came every month were in there, milling around, and we all said our polite hellos. The island in the kitchen was full of standard fruit platters and veggie trays that Greg had catered. A few of the ladies that came with their respective spouses always seemed to contribute too.

I held up my six-pack. "Let me put these on ice. You want one?"

"Nah. I don't drink."

I raised a brow at that, wondering how he would get along with the rest of us.

I turned around and headed the few steps to the kitchen, resigned to the fact that I wasn't lucky enough for Quinn to be gone. She stood at the center island with her back to me. Her ass was practically eating the tiny fucking shorts she was wearing, and my gaze followed the tanned skin of her legs down to her Converse shoes.

How could I ever tease her again? The way I had her entire life... before the incident. I could hardly swallow.

She looked like she was holding a glass up to the tap, which Greg and I had installed last summer. It had been a bitch to take out half the counter and install the keg and proper hosing equipment up through the granite.

Greg, Dustin, and a few other men stood on the opposite side of the island, watching Quinn pour a beer. She proffered the glass, half beer and half foam, to Dustin. "Apparently, tilting the glass is trickier than you let on," she said.

Dustin took the glass and raised it. "Not a problem. I love a lot of head."

"Don't. We. All." The words were out before I could think. My voice was low and husky, drawing each syllable out slowly. *Shit.*

Her shoulders went up, and Quinn turned around quickly. Our eyes locked on one another's. My fucking heart was like a Junior Jackson car from *The Last American Hero* hitting two hundred, but with her dad and everyone else standing around being an audience, I kept what emotion I could out of my eyes.

But Quinn's deep-green eyes widened in surprise. Her chest expanded while her bottom lip went into her mouth, and her cheeks turned a bright shade of pink. The look thrilled me. This was wrong on so many levels.

"Hey, Q." I nodded to Dustin and Greg, who were now laughing at something some of the other guys had said. "You'll get better at the whole less-head thing the more you pour." *Stop saying the word* head.

"What's your preference? Less head or more?" She raised an eyebrow at me knowingly.

This was not going how I planned. At. All.

A low chuckle escaped my throat, and her mouth went into a smirk. I wasn't sure what had happened during the three minutes from the time that I was parking my car—hoping to avoid all Quinn interactions—to me leaning forward and towering over her. She didn't move, and I made damn sure not to touch her. "I think you know the answer to that already."

"Come on, Quinn. The guys are waiting." Hannah broke the palpable tension between us, tugging Quinn out of the space between the counter and my hovering.

Laughing, Quinn allowed her friend to pull her toward the hallway in the opposite direction of the living room. Before she got too far, she turned back to me with a large grin on her face. "Maybe it will be different next time."

I slow-blinked. She had officially stumped me. Was she referring to my blowjob from Kimber?

"You want them on ice?" Dustin nodded toward my six-pack, breaking into my thoughts.

"Yes, give me a second. I'm getting to it."

"You weren't giving her too bad of a time about all the foam, were you?"

I started shoving the beer bottles into the ice, letting the cubes burn my fingers as I slid five bottles in. I needed to wake up from this mind fog. Dustin was right. In normal life —life two months ago—I would have given Quinn crap about not pouring properly. "No. Not at all. She doesn't drink that much."

Dustin lifted his glass to the tap and filled his half-empty glass with zero foam. "I didn't want to embarrass her."

Dustin was way too polite for that, but Quinn wasn't the easily embarrassed type. *Maybe it will be different next time.* Her words replayed themselves over and over in my head. Then I remembered I'd left the new guy in the living room and, wanting a reprieve from Dustin, made a quick dash away from Dustin's questioning gaze to my new friend. The guy didn't know me well enough to catch that I was freaking the fuck out about the small conversation I'd just had with Quinn.

I found Kevin standing on the front porch. He appeared to be using his hand, talking animatedly to someone. I pushed open the door and stuck my head out. My night was officially... weird.

"Jason." Kimber gave me a quick smile but continued to stare at me like I had something to say. Rather reluctantly, she gestured to Kevin. "Have you met Kevin? He and I went to college together."

"He is one of three people I've met so far," Kevin said. "I wasn't expecting to see my ex-girlfriend, though."

"It was a big mistake to break up with you." Kimber bowed her head then raised her chin, looking directly at Kevin. "Something we definitely don't need to involve Jason with."

Please don't. The weird flirty but forbidden sixty seconds I'd shared with Quinn was enough for one evening. I gave Kimber the warmest smile I could muster. "Absolutely," I said. "I'll leave you two alone to catch up." The screen door shut softly behind me.

After that, I didn't even have to avoid Kimber. An hour later, she and Kevin came inside, and she steered clear of me. Even though Quinn was gone, I couldn't completely relax, and no matter how many beers I drank—I'd had four —the tension in my neck was starting to give me a headache.

"What's up with you tonight? You've been out of sorts. I thought for sure when Randy started talking politics, you'd have something to say about the immigration policies." Greg tilted his beer toward mine, and I clinked my bottle to his glass.

"Nah. Didn't have enough energy to set him straight. Haven't been sleeping well. How's everything with you? Work? Home? Dating?" Unbelievable guilt was already eating at me, and I had done nothing to Quinn. Nothing physical anyway. Mental stimulation? I chugged the rest of my beer.

"You know me. Hospital is my life. Elizabeth's working in pediatrics now, so it's nice to see my daughter once in a while."

"If Christina ever gave me the time of day, it would be amazing," I said about my oldest daughter.

"Still blames you for the divorce?" he asked.

I nodded. I pretended to be over it at this point, but the pain in my chest could damn near topple me sideways. Holly and I had been married for twenty-one years before she requested a divorce. We were happy. Or so I'd thought. It was a perpetual ache that never went away—that I wasn't good enough to enjoy a long and healthy, happy life with the one woman who had known me better than anyone. "Amazing how Holly was entirely at fault, but somehow, my oldest, most-wisest daughter can't see the truth. Even when it's staring her in the face."

"Probably why she makes a good parole officer. I gotta be honest—it's been great having Quinn back in the house. Debra wasn't ever loud, but fuck, you can't imagine how quiet the house is without her."

I raised an eyebrow at Greg.

He nodded sheepishly. "Sometimes I forget that we've both lost someone. Just not the same way."

I shrugged. I didn't want the conversation to get too pitiful with us rehashing his loss and my ex. "What are

Quinn's plans? You know my door is always open for her. I know I've always said it, but I'm serious. Always have been."

"Even though you've told her that a million times, I'm not sure she's taken it seriously. Her bar exam is next week."

"Holy shit. Congrats! Good for her." I brushed a hand over my face. "God, I'm old. It's hard to believe Q is going to be a lawyer."

"Tell me about it. But she's always insisted she wants to do what you've always done. Real estate. Banking. All the boring shit. Been her mantra since she was ten."

I swallowed the guilt that kept wanting to resurface. I was surely going to hell for having these filthy thoughts of Quinn on her knees sucking my cock.

"She's confident she'll pass with flying colors," Greg said.

"Then what?"

He filled up his beer and handed me another one, placing my empty bottle on the counter, before turning back to me. The party was slowly dying out now. Only a few regulars sat around the living room.

I took a swig of beer, hoping it would wash away all my dirty thoughts.

"Then," Greg went on, "she'll be free to do what she wants. But you remember how it is. She won't know whether she passed until the first week in October. Soak up whatever knowledge she can get at the place she is working at now. Even though I think she wanted to talk to you about that."

"Me? Why?"

Just then, the woman in question strutted into the kitchen with Hannah and two young guys in tow. The taller kid was holding Quinn's hand, but the second she met my gaze, she let go like he was fire.

My heart did a weird thing.

"Quinn. Perfect timing. I was telling Jason about your bar exam next week. And your plans."

She pulled a strand of hair from her face while Hannah led the guys into the living room, talking about proving them wrong about something. I couldn't get the full conversation because my attention was focused entirely on Quinn. She'd changed shirts. She was wearing a royal-blue tank top that had strings laced up the front, so it caused the fabric to bunch together around her tits.

Quinn giggled. "Now, Dad? Really?"

"Quinn. What better time than the present?"

The strain of avoiding her chest was going to rip the skin under my eyes. I took another drink of my beer, hoping that it would make my voice sound normal because I sure as hell wasn't feeling remotely normal. "What's up, Q?"

She glanced away, not meeting my gaze right away. Was she embarrassed? She fisted her hands and uncurled them before she gripped the hem of her short shorts. "I was hoping with your recent vacancy at the firm, you would let me work for you." Her eyes flitted to her dad then back to me. "I won't get my bar results back until sometime in October—but I'll pass—then I was hoping I could work at your firm."

My eyes strayed. I blinked.

Shit.

She isn't wearing a bra.

3

QUINN

I should have just sent him a text. The situation was so awkward. Jason stood there for a full thirty seconds, staring at me like what I'd asked was a huge surprise. He's the one who'd always told me I could come work with him. Maybe he thought I wouldn't want anything to do with him after the blow job show.

My dad was buzzed, leaning against the arm of the love seat with a big grin on his face like his baby girl could do no wrong.

I went to open my mouth to say never mind, but Jason stood to his full height. "I've always told you my doors are open. In fact, I could really use you as a clerk—everything I don't have time for. Nothing that would require a license."

Just the sound of his voice sent my clitoris into alert mode. "I would love that. There is so much I want to learn from you. I could totally help you." *Sheesh, did I really say that all flirty?* I couldn't look at him anymore without seeing his pants unzipped and splayed across his lap, his rock-hard cock dripping with saliva. The worst part—best?—was that instead of Kimber kneeling in front of him, it was me. It was always me, the Q he'd been around since I was born. He was probably at the hospital celebrating with my dad when I came into this world.

"Why don't you stop by my office on Monday afternoon, and we can have a more in-depth conversation?" He lifted his beer bottle and gave me the boyish grin I'd seen a million times before. Only now, it sent my nerves into a tizzy.

"We can figure something out that will work for both of us," he said.

"See, Quinn? It wasn't that bad, was it?" My dad stood and wrapped his arm across my shoulder. "She's been talking about you non-stop this past month."

I frowned. "Have I? Probably because I've been so excited about becoming a lawyer." And it had nothing to do with how much I compared him and his sexual capabilities to the lame guys I knew. *Speaking of...* The basement light wasn't on, which meant there wasn't a soul down there. "Where's Kimber?"

Jason's eyes were twinkling. He was looking at me like he wanted to eat me. Or maybe I was projecting. My dad's best friend couldn't actually be attracted to me. Could he? I glanced at Billy, who was sitting on the floor on the far side of the living room, watching Hannah sort through my dad's Harry Chapin records. When I looked back at Jason, the look was still there. My knees trembled, and I couldn't stop blinking, thinking that I wanted Jason. Badly.

Given a choice between Billy and Jason? With Jason's solid arms and chest, the dimples when he smiled, and the way his eyes sparkled like he knew what I wanted and he could give it to me, there was no *thinking* I wanted Jason. I'd been fantasizing about Jason's mouth, hands, and cock for the past twenty-eight days. I wanted him more than I wanted my Jeep loan paid off.

"No clue where Kimber's at. I think she left with an old boyfriend she happened to meet up with here." Jason shrugged like he didn't care one way or the other. My heart soared.

"Oh." I put a hand to my chest, hoping to calm my heart, and when I did, Jason's gaze fell to my chest, as did mine. My nipples were hard, and even though the top had the scrunched-up ties against my chest, I could plainly see the points. That meant Jason could too...

A wave of heat rushed over my skin and down between my legs. Was the thermostat working? When I glanced back at Jason, he was no longer looking at me. Maybe I'd imagined it. Would it be awkward working at the same office? I would have to keep my distance. "Jason, I would love to come Monday." I cleared my throat. "Sorry I put you on the spot, and please don't feel like since we're family—" The glint in his eyes was back.

He chuckled and raised his beer to me. It felt like all the air had been sucked out of the room. He tipped his drink to my water. "Always here for you. Anything you need, Q, I'm the guy who can get it done."

Oh shit. My entire soul fell into Jason's bottomless blue eyes. My clit thrummed a happy beat as I leaned into his toast. "I know." Our drinks met, my knuckles brushed his, and my entire world shifted. I licked my bottom lip and slowly raised my eyes back to his. "And trust me, I'm going to hold you to it."

MONDAY CAME FASTER than a flash flood. I was a bundle of nerves the entire weekend. My ears pounded, and a headache was threatening at the base of my skull. In law school, I'd spent so many days imagining working with Jason. It was my dream. Besides my dad, he was the smartest guy around, and it would be the best thing to jumpstart my career. I had to give a winning interview. Even though I knew him, it was important to not act too casual.

I rolled my eyes. Fat chance when all I could think about was his dick in my mouth. I shook the thought to the back of my brain and focused on what I wanted my future to look like.

I'd followed Jason's career from the second I'd turned fifteen, and right then, I'd known without a doubt that I wanted to be a lawyer. In fact, the moment it had become crystal clear was when our families vacationed together at Jason's summerhouse, which was literally forty miles from my neighborhood, situated on an enormous lake. Everyone we came across adored Jason. He couldn't get out of any restaurant without someone greeting him or thanking him for representing so and so.

I slipped into my high heels and took one last glance in the mirror. I looked like a businesswoman. I looked exactly like a lawyer should look—I'd Googled that of course. I wore a black pencil skirt that stopped above my knees, paired with red shoes and a buttoned, red-collared top. I'd let my hair go au natural, so it lay in beachy waves over my shoulders.

I pulled into his lot and parked next to his black Lexus. I blew out a loud breath and checked my reflection in the rearview mirror to make sure I looked presentable. "This is just Jason." Not Jason with the fat, wet dick I wanted to slobber all over and have come in my mouth. *No, no, no.* "Don't start. This is business." I wiped beneath my eyes. "Business does not include wanting to fuck your potential boss. Do *not* think about the way his dick would feel sliding in and out of your mouth." *Great and now my cheeks are pink.*

My hand was clammy when I reached for the knob. I needed this job so much that I would have to forget any sexual tension between us after the good cock sucking I'd witnessed.

"May I help you?" A woman much older than me sat behind the front desk. She didn't smile, and it made my bundle of nerves even tighter. I'd been imagining a nice, welcoming face that would greet me and offer me a bottle of water.

"I'm Quinn. I'm here to see Jason."

She gave me a disapproving look, which was maddening. What was wrong with me? I was the picture-perfect professional.

"Mr. Richter is waiting for you. You need to walk down this hallway and turn right. His office is at the back of the building." Then as if she thought I needed it, she added, "There is a sign that says Jason Richter."

"Thank you." I headed off, happy to be rid of the grump. Would she change her tune when I started working here, or would she be one of those unlikable coworkers employees had to deal with?

Jason's office building was large and basic. I'd driven past it a million times but had never stepped foot inside. A few pictures of the mountains and some lakes decorated the hallway. Crazy images flashed through my head when I approached Jason's office—naughty images of him getting sucked off again while leaning on his desk, much like he had been in my bathroom.

At this rate, I should turn around and tell him I couldn't work for him. But his words—"Always here for you. Anything you need, Q, I'm the guy who can get it done for you"—made me keep going. I didn't want to think about whether he meant that sexually or professionally, and I tried to separate the two in my mind.

Thank God his door was closed. It gave me a second to compose myself. I knocked.

"Come in, Q." His deep, confident voice soothed over me.

This was Jason. I could totally do this. I pushed the door open and stood up ramrod straight. Jason was sitting in his chair with a phone pressed to his ear. He was wearing a pressed collared white shirt. The sleeves were rolled up, exposing his forearms. No tie meant no court today. I plastered on my best "I don't want you to read my emotions" face and gave him a small wave.

He winked.

I nearly died.

He gestured for me to sit, and I was so fucking nervous, I couldn't. I walked to the far side of his office, gazing at all the law books on his shelves. I especially loved the ladder attached to his bookshelf. There were wheels on the bottom so it could be rolled across the floor. The wood was smooth and cool beneath my grip, and I gave it a test push, but it wouldn't budge.

Jason's laughter echoed behind me, and I turned to find him standing, his eyes on me.

"Yes. I will be sure to do that. It's always a pleasure working with you. Thank you." Jason ended the call and gave me the biggest, most beautiful smile I'd ever seen. "Awesome bookshelf, isn't it?"

He was so good at breaking the tension, and I loved him for that. He was normal Jason. "Yes! I tried moving it, but it wouldn't budge."

He bent down and flipped a little metal piece against the wheel. "Comes with brakes. That way, I don't fall and break my neck when I'm up top." He straightened. "Now try."

I pushed the ladder, making it glide across the hardwood floor a few feet. "I want this." I laughed.

"Would you like a tour of the building? Do you want to see the empty office before we talk about specifics?"

How was this the same man I'd seen getting head? He was so professional and calm. His confidence was admirable. "I would love to. Please. Show me the way."

"Fantastic. I'll show you what could potentially be your office first, and we can go from there."

We walked directly across the hall, and he opened the door. There was a desk and chair matching the ones in Jason's office. It was an exact replica of his room, including the empty bookshelf—and ladder.

"It has a ladder too? I love it."

"We can do this a handful of ways. I know you do all the research where you are now. I would kill to have you working for me doing that same thing while you're waiting for your exam results."

"I would love to be here. I wished it would have worked out sooner. Tell me more."

"Then in October, once you have your license, I would give you all the crap cases that I don't want to deal with, and I would expect you to toe the line. You could be my associate. Or the second option would be that you rent this office out and have your own clientele. In which case, you'd pay rent—"

"How much is rent?"

He gave a dry laugh. "More than you could afford in the beginning would be my guess. My preference would be that we work as a team, and I would essentially be your mentor and allow you to build up a client base. I'd provide you the freedom to build up your own clientele with the expectation that you wouldn't steal mine at a later date when you're ready to branch out on your own." He unlocked the brake on the ladder for me to test drive it. "Providing you had free time to take on other clients once you're a full-blown lawyer."

Full-*blown* lawyer. I couldn't keep the smirk off my face. Just hearing him say the word... I pursed my lips. "What makes you think I'd do that? Steal your clients." I gripped the ladder and moved it to the far-left side.

"You're a millennial. And a rebel. You keep everyone on their toes with your actions."

"Rude," I said. "Plus, I barely made the cutoff to be a millennial, so I wouldn't put much stock into that." I pushed the ladder across the room, imagining the shelves filled with books upon books like in Jason's office. "If you were anyone but you, I'd be offended."

"I get it. But I know you. So I speak the truth."

It wasn't like I tried to be a rebel. There were things I strongly believed in and stood up for. Obviously, there were things I'd done and had major regrets about. "You do." I conceded, not in the least offended. "What did you do when you were first starting out?"

"Worked with my grandfather. It took a long fucking time to build what you're looking at today. There are two types of lawyers, Quinn. Those that don't mind being the employee and those that are in charge." He shrugged. "It's your choice which one you want to be."

He walked away, leaving my mouth hanging open. Who knew Jason could be so profound?

I followed him to the door, but he turned back so abruptly, we smacked into one another. His hands went to my hips, steadying me. *Holy moly*. My muscles went slack, my skin hyperaware of his proximity. I was literally putty in his hands. He smelled phenomenal. It was a heady combination of dangerous adventure and smooth whiskey.

"Quinn, can we stop beating around the bush and get straight to the point?"

4

JASON

Her throat shifted when she swallowed. Her scent had been swirling in the air since she'd walked into my office, and not for the first time, I imagined her smooth skin pressed against my nose and mouth.

"You mean what I saw between you and Kimber?"

"We were never dating. It was just a thing a few times." *Fuck. Why did I say that to her? Like I owe her any explanation?*

Quinn's hips felt amazing beneath my hands, and when she licked her lips, I removed my hands. I couldn't do this if we were going to work together. Well, I couldn't do this at all because her dad was my best friend.

"Billy and I aren't dating either. Not that you probably care. But just FYI. And I never did that to him so... yeah." Red marred her cheeks, and she looked out the office window.

Relief coursed through me. I appreciated that she hadn't given a guy like Billy head. But this was not the route I should be taking. "Listen. I'm sorry you were exposed to that. I appreciate that you didn't say anything to Greg about it."

Quinn gave me her rebel look. "Don't put kid gloves on me. It wasn't that big of a deal. Like I'm ever going to tell my dad I watched you get your cock sucked. Watched you come inside Kimber's mouth. Seriously. Or that you've seen me in my bra."

I had semi-wood the second Quinn uttered the words *your cock*. It was crazy. And definitely something we couldn't act on. Even if I wanted to. *Shit.*

"I should apologize for standing there like a pervert and watching you."

"How long did you watch?" The words were out of my mouth before I could think of any true consequences. I was in dangerous territory. But it felt good.

Her tongue came out and licked her bottom lip. "Not long enough."

Her answer caught me off guard, and I chuckled. "Not the answer I was expecting, but okay." I tiptoed out of where this was headed. "Let's go check out the rest of the building. It takes a while before Leona will soften to you, so we better get started on that if you're going to be working here every day."

"The crabby woman at the desk?"

"The one and only. But you better not say that to her face. She's been known to make people's lives hell."

"Maybe she needs to have some sexual release. That would brighten her mood immensely."

I shook my head. But Quinn had me smiling.

Could I work with Quinn? Her bold attitude and even bolder actions made her a semi-loose cannon, and the fact that she would be representing Richter, Richter & Salazar made me a tad nervous. She was very intelligent, and with the proper training, Quinn would no doubt turn into a phenomenal lawyer someday.

I pointed to an open door. "Kitchen and break room. There are two other attorneys here. Wilson Richter was my grandfather, hence the 'Richter, Richter' part. And Juan Salazar is my partner. If you're still here when he gets back, I'll introduce you. Then Sabrina Wilson, but she's on vacation for another week." We moved down the hall, and I pointed to the two closed doors that were Jessica's and Bobbi's offices. "Two of three paralegals—one works from home—are in there. And you've already met Leona."

I led the way down the hall with Quinn walking slowly behind me. Once inside my office, I gestured for her to sit. When she didn't, I said, "So the bar is this week?"

"On Thursday." Quinn gave a hearty sigh. "I could really see myself working here and learning from the best. I've always been fascinated by you and the relationships you've developed with everyone around town."

"I wouldn't say I'm the best. But it helps that we already have a relationship. Why don't you take a few days to think about what I'm offering you and give me a call."

"No."

"No?" I asked. "Because of what you saw?"

"No. I loved what I saw." She put emphasis on the word *loved*.

"Quinn," I said in warning. I was close to being on the edge. Every fiber of my being wanted to touch her, to truly live in this moment with this young, vibrant woman who'd freaking watched me come inside another woman's mouth and wasn't sickened by it. I wanted to see what the other side of my single life had in store for me after being a loyal married man for twenty-three years and two months. It was *so* wrong. But a part of me didn't really care.

"Don't 'Quinn' me. You have to promise me something."

I hesitated. "I don't know if I can. What?"

"If I work here, you have to treat me like an adult woman. No 'Quinning' me. No trying to decide what's best for me. No trying to tell me that I shouldn't *love* seeing you the way I did."

"You want me to treat you like any other colleague that I work with?" Did it occur to her that I didn't sleep or flirt with any of the folks I worked with?

Her eyes flashed. "I wouldn't say that entirely. We do have a relationship, and it will serve me well to lean on that. I don't want what you're trying to do right now."

"What am I trying to do?"

Quinn stepped toward me and put a hand to her hip. "You're trying to brush off what I saw as something that I shouldn't find appealing. Like I'm not an old enough woman to experience the enjoyment of a good cock sucking."

For once in my life, I couldn't think of anything to say. Quinn's green eyes were blazing so brightly, it was hard to determine whether it was out of anger, arousal, or both. "You're maddening. It's nothing to do with that. And stop saying the word *cock*."

Her mouth tipped up into her rebel grin. "Why?"

"Because... it's... unprofessional," I lied.

"Really, Jason? I secretly think you like hearing me say it. Cock. Cock. Cock. *Your* cock." Her eyes went to my khakis, where my cock was about to make himself known. "You know, when I was watching you—"

I put a hand to her mouth. I couldn't take anymore. *Am I the only one who's trying to be good?*

Her eyes flashed in victory. Her nostrils flared.

"Don't tell me. I thought we were putting this behind us and moving forward?"

I kept my hand over her mouth, and a rush of wild heat flooded through my system at the way Quinn's chest heaved, her eyes softened, and her shoulders went limp. Attraction sizzled off the charts between us. Then her tongue came out and wet my hand.

"What the hell?" I laughed and pulled my hand away.

Again, she smirked. "That's exactly what I mean. You wouldn't ever do that to Kimber, would you?" She held up the hand that she'd licked. "Plus, I never said I was putting anything behind us. *You* want that."

She had a valid point about not doing that to Kimber. But how did I explain that I'd covered her mouth because I *wanted* to hear what she had to say, and I *shouldn't* want that? I was getting closer to the ledge and into her space. "Kimber is not my best friend's twenty-five-year-old daughter. And I know you better than her." I shook my head. "What are you doing, Q?"

"You don't feel this between us?" Quinn gestured with her hand.

I weighed my options. I could be honest and direct and hope that this would go away if I was. Or I could lie. Lying was the best route in all of this. Nothing would come of this anyway. She might have enjoyed what she'd seen, but that didn't mean I was the object of her attraction—just the image that presented itself to her was her attraction.

"You saw me getting my dick sucked. That doesn't constitute that there is something between us."

"Yes or no question, Counselor."

I put my arms across my chest. "I think we both got caught up in the moment of that—"

"Incident."

"Yeah. Incident. I'm forty-six, Q. Recently divorced. I have kids around your age. Not to mention the fact that I've been around you since you were born. I'm like an uncle of sorts."

She put her hand up in a stop gesture. "What is your point?"

I groaned. "Why are you being so difficult?"

She opened her mouth in shock. "I'm not. You're hardly letting me talk. Which goes back to my original request. If I work here and take this beautiful office with its adorable little book ladder—I'm gonna need books by the way, for research—I can't have you treating me like a child. Or like you're my protector. I'm not even proposing anything, and you're already like"—she put her arms up in a gesture like she was running—"Q, I'm forty-six. Recently divorced."

I laughed at her deep voice as she tried to imitate me. "Fine. For the next two minutes, we can have it your way. What are you saying that I'm not letting you say?" My nerve endings were spiking out of control. I couldn't imagine what might come out of her mouth. Her lips were flushed pink like someone had kissed them, and her cheeks weren't far behind being rosy.

She stepped closer to me and laid her hand flat against my chest. My heart *thud-thud, thud-thud, thud-thud*ded against her palm. Her eyes burned heat through my skin, and I didn't want to tear my gaze away from her hand because I was afraid. I was afraid my wobbly walls would crumble under her compelling gaze. But she was intense, drawing me in without saying a word.

My gaze met hers. We held still like that for countless seconds. The beats in my heart quickened with every second, probably echoing through the room. She was beautiful. I'd never noticed the multiple shades of green in her eyes or the way she commanded attention through them.

Her mouth went up into a small grin that sent my entire body into overdrive. *What is happening to me?*

She wiggled her fingers against my heart. "This proves that there is something between us."

I stayed silent.

"When I was watching Kimber suck your cock, it was so hot. So filthy. You were so powerful and confident standing there, but you were also a man almost at his breaking point. It was the most erotic thing I've ever seen in my life. It didn't help that minutes before, I was already thinking about how handsome you were. Something shifted in me that night. My eyes and my heart changed. I saw you for the man you are. And the whole time I watched Kimber suck your cock, there was only one thing going through my mind." She paused, and her hand traveled down the length of my chest and stomach. She skimmed her palm across my erection.

She gave me a knowing grin. "All I could think about was how badly I wanted that to be me."

5

QUINN

Jason took a large step back. The look on his face was a mix of arousal and pain. *What did I do?* He was aroused. He was attracted to me. "You've thought about it too? Haven't you?"

"I, uh... look, Quinn—"

"Oh, so it's Quinn now?"

"Don't make me fire you before you even get hired, little girl."

I put a hand to my hip. "Stop. Treating. Me. Like. A. Child."

Jason didn't give me one of his real smiles when he grinned. "Stop acting like one, then. Don't pull that shit on me. Your dad would flip if he knew you just did that."

"You gonna tell him?"

My question was answered with silence.

"Thought so. Am I mistaken that you want me too? You're hard as hell. And you never answered me. In fact, you haven't answered any of my questions."

He struggled to find the right words, and I wanted to laugh at this flustered Jason. Finally, he released a breath. "You don't want to give me head. It was the *idea*—the image

—that was imprinted on your brain that makes you *think* you're attracted to me."

"Like watching porn or something and having a crush on the male lead?"

Jason laughed. "Yes."

I shook my head and clenched my hands into fists. It was like he hadn't heard a word I'd said about not treating me like a child. This wasn't like watching freaking porn or anything else. I wanted him.

"Why are you denying this? You are frustrating me beyond belief. Stop telling me how I should feel. Please, for like five minutes, can you be real with me? Be honest with me. And respect what I'm feeling."

He was already shaking his head. The urge to push him in the chest was so strong, I found myself inches from his beautiful face. His eyes said so many things—all the things his mouth wasn't saying. But something swirled between us. Something strong and undeniable. I didn't want to let this out of my grasp.

I placed my hands loosely against his shoulders and chest. "Don't tell me no. Who is acting like a child now? Not using their words?"

That comment garnered a genuine laugh from him. When Jason laughed, his dimples came out, so sexy and boyish at the same time. It made my stomach flutter like I was racing down a large hill and wasn't quite to the bottom.

"You're twenty years younger than I am, Quinn."

"I know. But it doesn't mean you shouldn't let me think the way I want. And feel the things I feel. You've been doing it our whole meeting—not trusting my judgment. Forget the cock-sucking incident. I can't work for you if you're not going to trust my choices, my gut, my instincts."

He nodded. "That's fair. I apologize. I'll try to let it go

and trust your decisions. It's an adjustment looking at you in a different way."

"Thank you." I appreciated his sincerity. I squeezed his shoulders and gave him my biggest smile. "Now, I want to know what was going through your mind when you saw me standing in my room watching you."

He chuckled. "I am not telling you. I'm not stepping over that line, Quinn. Your dad would kill me. Not to mention the fact that you'll soon be working with me, and that is an equally sized line that I don't step over."

I put my hands on my hips. "You liked it."

He stepped away and walked around to his desk. "I'll have you know this is no way to start a working relationship. I'm gonna be your boss."

Yummy. Boss and my dad's best friend? But that wasn't what he wanted to hear. "Okay, well, I'm glad we cleared the air. I feel better." I smiled. "I know we'll make a great team."

I had to go along with this. I couldn't risk him not hiring me. Meanwhile, it was going to be fun. I was confident we could remain professional on the outside and when working cases, but when we were alone... I wanted Jason all to myself. I wanted him to show me what it was like in bed with a man like him. How he would taste. How he would pleasure me. The kinds of things he liked. The experience he had. All the things I craved.

"Stop looking at me like that." Jason's deep voice brought me out of my trance.

He had a wild side, and I wanted to soak it all up.

"Do you want to know what I was thinking?"

"No." His eyes were saying yes.

"Fine." I shrugged. "I have to give my two-week notice

at the firm. Will that be okay with you for me to start here, then?"

"Fine by me."

"Can I start moving my stuff over here?"

"Sure." He pulled out a silver key. "I'll let you have this key to bring stuff over as you have time. For now, you can use any of my books you might need in my office until you purchase your own. Call me once you've taken the exam. I'm excited to hear how you think you did."

"But it'll be weeks before I get my results back. Colorado is at a ten-week turnaround for results, and then if I fail, I literally have to reschedule right away to take the next one in February."

He set the key on his desk. "You'll do great, Q. You're intelligent. You'll pass."

I rubbed my hands together. "Oh, this is going to be so much fun. Working with the best. You know, maybe someday it will be Richter, Salazar & Brenning. Thank you, thank you for this opportunity. You won't be disappointed, Jason." I skipped around his desk and threw my arms around his neck, squeezing him tightly with gratitude. "I love you, Jason. I'll be forever grateful for this. You know that, right?"

Jason's hands slowly circled my hips. He hugged me back. "I know. Love you too, Q." His voice was low and heavy, making my brain swirl with desire. My clit thrummed with excitement and this heady arousal of Jason. He felt amazing against my body. I kept my arms around his neck and leaned back so I could look into his eyes. His eyes were stormy blue and held that spark of attraction I'd noticed before.

My eyes dropped to his lips. His lips were perfect. He

didn't have a cupid's bow; it was flat across the top. But they were perfect. How would they feel against my skin?

My chest thumped. I wished he would get over my dad being his best friend and agree to explore the sexual tension between us.

Kiss me, Jason.

He was shaking his head as if I'd said it aloud. He slowly released me from his hold, and I stepped back. "You're going to be the death of me, Q."

IT WASN'T until I was brushing my teeth for bed that night that I realized Jason hadn't given me the key like he'd said he would. It wasn't a big deal right now, but I hauled out my phone to text him anyway.

Electricity zinged through my nerves. I'd texted him once or twice even though I'd had his number for ages. It was pushing eleven o'clock. Would he be awake?

Me: *Hey. Thank you for meeting me today. I am so excited to work for you. Also, you forgot to give me a key.*

I slid between my sheets, my fingers already aching from clutching my phone like it was life or death if he texted me back. Maybe he wouldn't take the bait. What a day. All horniness aside, working for Jason was my dream come true. My biggest dream was to be his partner. That would be the icing on the cake, and yes, I had zero clientele to pull in any billable hours right now. I was confident I would soon enough, though. I would take whatever I could get at this point.

My phone hadn't buzzed with a message yet. *Please text me back, Jason.* I could still feel the beat of his heart against my fingertips. The look in his eyes had told me how badly he wanted me. It'd been floating in my head all freaking day. That, and the look he'd given me when he caught me watching him getting sucked off. Tingles shot up my spine.

I was soaking wet, and like I'd been doing since last month, I started rubbing circles around my clit, wishing it was Jason's large fingers. What would Mr. Big Shot think if I sent him a picture of me touching myself right now? Would he ignore it?

My phone lit up next to me, and Jason's name flashed across the screen.

Jason: *You're right. I can leave it with Leona, and you can swing by anytime to pick it up.*

Me: *I'd rather get it directly from you.*

Jason: *Fine. We can meet tomorrow sometime, or I can come by the house. Don't you have to work in the morning? Why aren't you in bed?*

I laughed.

Me: *It's only 11:11 and I am in bed...*

I wanted to scream because he was so adorable, and I could perfectly envision the look on his face as he thought about me in bed.

The little bubbles on my phone popped up then disappeared, and I waited patiently for them to reappear. They did. I really wanted to tell him how turned on I was. But he was nervous. He needed finessing. I would have to go slow to get what I wanted.

Jason: *I should go to bed too.*

Me: *Don't go. Talk to me. Send me a picture. How was the rest of your day after I left?*

Again, my phone went dark. I was restless. I wanted...

Jason: *Not bad. How was your day?*

I was disappointed that he'd ignored my request for a photograph.

Me: *Good. Can I send you a picture of myself?*

Jason: *Are you fully clothed?*

Me: *Do you want me to be?*

Jason: *Q... I can't go down this road with you.*

Me: *No one will ever find out. Think of all the fun we would have together.*

Jason: *We are going to work together.*

Me: *So?*

Me: *I'm going to send you a picture now. My clit has been throbbing all day thinking about you touching it. And I know, Jason... I can feel it, that you've been thinking about me too.*

My fingers trembled. I pulled the sheet down, exposing my nakedness. Seduction play numero uno. I spread my legs and snapped a picture from my stomach down. The lighting wasn't bright but not dark enough that he wouldn't be able to see. Without a second thought, I hit Send.

My heart raced. I began touching myself again. It was going to be easy making myself orgasm, thinking of Jason's strong hands touching my body. What was he thinking right now, looking at my text?

He would look.

He wouldn't delete it.

Would he acknowledge it?

I arched my back. My orgasm rolled out of me in waves, while Jason's large hands and broad shoulders, his face and beautiful dimples, flashed through my mind.

My phone lit up. My heart stilled at what he might have typed back.

Jason: *You're beautiful, Q. And persistent. :-) You've given me a lot to think about.*

6

JASON

I jacked off to the picture Quinn had sent me last night. I was a man with no shame. I was back to being a pervert. Until the lights turned on.

I quickly ordered a chai from the barista at the drive-thru and hurried to my office. Quinn would be meeting me there.

What would the harm be in having an affair with Quinn if no one found out? I would carry guilt for the rest of my life from going behind my best friend's back. But the feeling Quinn had given me last night when she sent that naughty photo was priceless. Young. Wild. Carefree. Weirdly, I felt whole and wanted. For the first time in a long time, I felt alive.

Every time I pulled it up on my phone, the feeling that sang through my limbs and to my groin was addictive. And Quinn was beautiful. The stirring between us was something I'd never felt before. Maybe I had experienced it with Holly, but I sure couldn't remember.

Butterflies soared in my stomach when I spotted

Quinn's Jeep in my parking lot. Everything inside of me wanted to do this with her. Everything.

I slid my car next to hers and stepped out. She was leaning against the wall of my building, holding a to-go coffee cup from the place down the street.

"Hey, Q."

Her cheeks were pink. Her lips quirked up into a grin. Was she thinking about that impossibly sexy photo too?

"Good morning. I brought you a drink. I know chai is your favorite, but you might like this too."

"Thank you." I took a sip. Should I acknowledge the picture? Say thank you? I didn't know. "Hmm. This is good. Come on. Key is inside."

Once I punched in the code, I stepped aside, giving Quinn access first. She didn't share a look with me when she passed. I didn't take my eyes off her. She smelled like Skittles—just the way she had yesterday in my office—and it took everything in me not to reach out and pull her against me to savor her sweetness.

"You know, you could give me the code." Quinn winked.

"I have to get you a personal code setup, and I haven't had time to do that yet. Hence, the key, in the meantime. Follow me."

The door swooshed shut softly behind us. I was hyper-aware of Quinn walking behind me down the hallway. I'd never been this fucked up about anything in my life. All the times I'd offered Quinn a job at my firm, all the times I'd seen her in a bathing suit while playing with Cera and Christina, and now she was sending me nudes. A nude. One that was enough to bring me to my knees.

I would like to think of myself as a good man. I toed the

line. Made the proper choices. I was a good father. A good friend.

I swallowed and inserted my personal office key into the lock at my door. The lock clicked in the overbearing silence.

"Come in." A frog was stuck in my throat.

Behind me, Quinn gave a soft laugh.

I went straight to my desk and opened the top drawer to retrieve the single key for Quinn. I set my chai down and took off my suit coat. I had court all day today.

"You look great." Quinn's voice was soft and smooth. There were so many things I was noticing about her that I'd seen my whole life. It was both exasperating and intriguing.

I met her gaze and smiled. "Thanks. So do you."

She had on a pair of black slacks that stopped at her ankles and a white blouse. She was wearing a bra today, but it had to be super thin because I could see the hint of a nipple at her right breast. Her hair was pulled back. I wanted it down, swirling around her face.

Better to grip while she sucks my cock.

That little rebellious grin of hers made an appearance, and her hand went to her hip like she was in charge. It was cute. Little did she know that it was me who had the upper hand because even if I succumbed to her wishes, she would succumb to all of mine in the bedroom.

"Thinking about the picture I sent you?"

I laughed. "Hard not to. Forty-six years old, and that's the first picture of its kind I've ever gotten."

"Really?" Quinn bounced on her heels.

I nodded.

She snapped her fingers. "I'm gonna send you more. Not sure when, but stay tuned." She wiggled her eyebrows up and down. "Unless you're ready to see the real thing in person."

The top button of her blouse was already open, and her hands went to the second button like she was going to undress.

I shook my head. "You wouldn't. Leona will be here any minute."

"You know I will." She flicked open the second button.

My cock stirred to life, thinking about the shirtless Quinn I'd seen in the basement. Plus, she was right. I *knew* she would do it. I took the few steps across my office, key in hand, and stopped in front of her. "Quinn..."

"Don't 'Quinn' me." *Pop!* Another button.

My fucking knees trembled. "Are you normally this forward with all of your... men?"

She arched her neck and laughed like I'd said the funniest thing in the world. Her beauty stung me. My fingers itched to pull her to me.

I raised my hand to do just that when Leona's voice floated through my office. "Greg is waiting for you on line two. He said it'll be quick."

Quinn's eyes widened, whereas I settled back down to reality, my dick deflating like a balloon slowly losing its air. I kept eye contact with Quinn and said to Leona, "Thanks. I'll pick it up."

"Don't say it," Quinn said to me.

But we both knew I didn't need to. As enticing as she was... "This is my fucking reality, Q. Your dad would cut my nuts off."

I DIDN'T HEAR from Quinn that night, but the next night, I got a text while I was drying off from a shower after the gym. Her first text was sweet and innocent.

Quinn: *Thanks for this opportunity. I really cannot wait to work with you side by side.*

Quinn: *You might get tired of seeing me so much!*

Happiness threatened to burst my chest wide open. I caught my reflection in the mirror. I wasn't the worst-looking guy out there, but yeah, I was aging. My chest hair was almost thoroughly gray. I had fine lines around my eyes, and there wasn't a day that went by that I didn't have a thought in one room and forget it by the time I got to the next room.

My physique rivaled most young dudes', though, and I still had a full head of hair, which was still brown. Mostly. I leaned in closer to the mirror. So what if there were areas of gray sprinkled throughout when the lighting hit it just right? I had two good bonuses as far as I could tell. I wasn't quite fifty yet, and I could still get it up. What did young Quinn find so appealing in me that Holly had lost interest in?

I picked up my phone and texted Q back.

Me: Not a chance. You're stuck with me.

I added the word *kid* out of habit but quickly deleted it. We had established she was no *kid* anymore.

Quinn: *I keep trying to tell you that that is EXACTLY where I want to be.*

I chuckled to myself. My phone vibrated with another text.

Quinn: *Send me a picture. What are you doing right now? Watch this.*

I'd sent selfies to the girls before, just silly dad stuff, but I'd never sent a selfie in the interest of sexual attention. It took another minute before her picture came through.

Only it wasn't a picture—it was a video. She was wearing a tiny pink spaghetti-strap tank top, and her hair was down, floating around her shoulders the way I loved. She was smiling.

I hit Play. Quinn's voice filled the room.

"Hey. I have been having the best few months of my life. The best last few days. Seeing you. Knowing I'll be working with you. It's taken all my thoughts away from not being there when my mom died. I haven't felt this alive in so long, Jason. Let's do this together. You will not regret it. Well, at least I hope you wouldn't. I sure won't. Come on." She proceeded to bite her lip, then a naughty smile crossed her face, and she pulled down her top, exposing her perfect little tits.

My stomach dipped in a good, healthy way. My dick went from semi-wood to fucking flagpole while I watched Quinn trace her pink nipples with her fingertips. She raised her gaze back to the camera. Desperate need washed over me when I saw the look in her eyes. It was like she could see me as if we were on a video chat and not pre-recorded.

"I want you to do this to me, Jason. Only you. There are so many dirty secrets I want to have with you that I've been too ashamed to admit to anyone else."

Fuck.

I slowly stroked my cock and gave it a full tug. Then another one. I would explode if she touched me, let alone have her tight pussy sheathing my dick. She paused then shimmied her tank top completely off her arms, so it was wrapped around her waist. She flung her bedsheet off, the camera going wobbly for a second. Then the video stilled. She sat with her knees bent and spread, exposing her fucking perfectly shorn pussy.

That was when my decision was made. No going back.

I was going to eat that perfect juicy pussy no matter what it cost me.

7

QUINN

I didn't text Jason after the video. Not the next day or the next. Not even after I took my bar exam. That was hard because I was pretty sure I'd done really well on it, and I was so excited to tell him about it. But I didn't text. All week, I had been stockpiling stuff to move into Richter, Richter & Salazar because I'd been too busy to make it back over there between dinner with my dad and Elizabeth, then I went with Hannah to her parent's dinner party.

The traffic lights couldn't change faster. I was dying to see Jason. It was time to lay it all on the line. We were doing this, or we weren't. He would do it. though. I could feel it in my bones.

When my mom was sick and had her hysterectomy, I'd known the doctors hadn't removed all the cancer. Even though her doctor was so happy with the results and so confident that she'd "gotten everything," I'd known she hadn't.

I hadn't known that. But I'd *felt* it—the second that door opened and the doctor was all happy. It was a lie that I wasn't even a part of. But I knew.

In the firm's parking lot, I loosened my grip on the steering wheel. I pulled up next to a really nice Rolls Royce. Jason's Lexus was parked on the other side of the Rolls, and I chuckled at the thought of what he would think if I sent him a picture of me naked sprawled against his car.

I was very tempted to do it, even in broad daylight, but the fact that I would be working here and there was a client inside took priority. I smiled. *Look at me acting like a professional instead of a nude model.*

I hauled a tub of books and personal file folders from the back of my Jeep and headed inside. The plaque on the wall—Richter, Richter & Salazar—would have to be replaced if I ever made partner. Richter, Brenning & Salazar. That had a nice ring to it.

"Eeeekkk! So exciting."

Jason's door was closed, prohibiting me from seeing him. My clit was hyperaware of the low hum of his voice. My office smelled like it had been recently disinfected. Jason must have made sure it was sparkly clean before I moved in even though it had looked brand-new the day of our meeting.

I immersed myself in unpacking and arranging things the way I wanted. Evening turned into darkness. My blood pumped loudly in my ears when I heard Jason's door shut. His key was ultraloud in the lock.

My door creaked open. Then Jason's large body filled my doorway. His hand was stroking his tie. His eyes were dark and dangerous. His mouth curved up into a grin. "I haven't heard from you. You take your test?"

Those damn dimples.

"Yeah. It went well." My voice was fraught with nerves. I had a quick panic attack, thinking he was going to tell me no.

"Thought you might have changed your mind." He stepped inside my office and pushed the door shut.

I swallowed. "Never."

He inched closer to me. His eyes raked over me. Shivers traveled up my spine, and the cup of pens in my hand shook, so I set them down on my desk. He moved into my personal space and put his hands on my desk, locking me between his arms.

I sucked in a deep breath. Jason's mouth crashed into mine, stealing that breath. *Oh, fuck.* I slid my tongue into his mouth. A low guttural growl escaped from his throat. I wrapped my arms around his neck, trying to devour him. To show him how badly I wanted this.

His mouth was hot, and his tongue was blessedly skilled, meeting my kisses and nibbles in sync. My panties were soaked, and if he touched me, I would explode without much effort. I pushed my hips into his erection, and the next thing I knew, Jason's strong hands were lifting me, so I sat at the edge of my desk, my legs dangling over the side with Jason's body between them.

He pulled back and cupped my cheeks with his hands, his eyes stared into my soul. "You make me feel alive." He nipped my bottom lip. "We have to keep this a secret from everyone, Quinn."

I nodded.

"Especially Greg and my girls."

"I know." I wanted this so bad, I would do whatever was necessary to make it happen. I had no intentions of telling Hannah, even though I pretty much told her everything in my life. "Tell me what you want. How I can make you happy."

Jason smiled and slid his hands down my neck, trailing

the straps of my tank top against my chest. "I don't want to ruin this moment by talking."

He slipped my top down beneath my breasts. My nipples tightened in the cool room. His warm fingertips glided across both hard pebbles. I sucked in a breath. His gaze followed the path of his fingers from my nipples and over the small piece of cloth to the wide expanse of my stomach. Goosebumps peppered my skin.

"You're beautiful, Q." He let out a little chuckle. "There is a high probability of me exploding too fast with you." His fingers moved around in slow, teasing caresses against my belly.

"I don't care. I know you'll take care of me. I haven't wanted anything this bad in such a long time."

He dropped his hands and stepped back, leaving my body cool and lonely. He loosened his tie in one firm tug. The movement was so sexy, so ethereal, that I was certain I had fallen and hit my head. Perhaps I *was* in the hospital hallucinating, or I was in heaven.

"What's the matter?" he asked.

"I've waited months for this, and now that you're standing in front of me... what if I can't meet your sexual demands? I'm nervous. Maybe I bit off more than I can chew."

Jason gave me a lopsided grin, and when his dimples appeared, I touched the little indents like I'd always wanted to. I couldn't stop staring at him. My heart was so full of this attraction... full of what was to come between us.

"That's not the Q I know. Where is that little rebel? The one who said—and I quote—'so many dirty secrets I want to try with you that I've been too ashamed to admit to anyone else.' I've got to tell you, I've been dying to see that part of you."

I swallowed. "You remembered exactly what I said?"

"No, baby. I watched your video so many times, your voice is on constant replay in my head."

I lunged into his arms, knowing he could take the impact and steady us. His arms went around my middle, and my lips sought his. Greedy lust enveloped my entire body, and I knew I would be safe with Jason and all of my dirty secrets. He would give me everything I wanted.

His cock was harder than I would have thought possible, and I ground myself into him. He was so much better than the young guys I dated. Just the feel of his large body, his apt hands squeezing my ass cheeks, and the way he let me devour his mouth without judgment was everything I needed. Everything I wanted.

I pulled back, unsure of what we were going to do in this moment, and Jason must have seen the questions in my eyes because he dropped to his knees and buried his face into my waist. "I can't wait to devour your fucking pussy. I'm going to destroy it."

I flicked the button on my jean shorts, and Jason pulled the zipper apart in one quick zip. He pulled my shorts down while he peppered my hips and pelvis with hot wet kisses.

"Please." That was all I could say because yes, that was what I wanted from Jason. I wanted him to devour me. I wanted him to destroy my pussy. It was all his, and I couldn't wait for him to give it to me.

Both of his hands ripped my thin panties directly down the middle of my legs, and I let out a laugh when he glanced up at me. I've never seen Jason like this. Playful. Happy. Horny. Between my clitoris and my heart, I wasn't sure which one was beating faster.

He pressed his nose against my skin where my pussy started to part. "You smell like my wildest dreams, Q."

I gripped his head and nudged it between my legs, unable to take it anymore. "I need you," I whispered.

He opened his mouth, his tongue lapping against my hard-as-hell pleasure point.

Jeez-us.

We were a crazy mixture of fast and slow. Soft but hard. He was demanding but gracious. I floated in clouds while his mouth made love to my pussy. The sounds of his mouth against my skin echoed around the room. When he thrust his fingers inside me, wave after wave of euphoria raced through my body. My mind was thoughtless, drifting in a sea of Jason and his paradise. He nipped my clit again, and I jumped. It was a live wire, ready to spark again at the smallest touch.

I opened my eyes and looked down at him. Jason was gorgeous. Manly. But when Jason gave me the most amazing smile of his, my come all over his lips, this Jason was my favorite. He made it difficult to breathe. I would die an old woman, married to someone who would probably never look at me the way this man was looking at me now.

"Did that just happen?" I asked stupidly.

He chuckled and stood, his mouth still glistening with my come. Then he leaned into me, placing his wet lips against mine. I reached for his bulging cock.

Thud, thud, thud.

Jason and I both jumped to attention. "Jason? You in there? I think the break room refrigerator is leaking."

Leona. Crap. My panties were in shreds. But where in the hell were my shorts?

8

JASON

"Court is adjourned."

Thank fuck. Never in my life did I think it would be this hard to concentrate on my job. Although, never in my life was I playing games with someone twenty years younger than I was either. And never in my life had I let something as simple as dating occupy my every waking moment as much as it had.

I practically tossed my legal work into my briefcase. My phone started ringing, and I used that as a reason to excuse myself from some colleagues.

"This is Jason."

"You working?" Greg's voice slowed my gait.

"Just got done. You calling from the hospital?"

"Yeah. You have a minute?"

I swallowed. "Sure do."

"I wanted to have a surprise dinner for Quinn. Just a little get-together. But I wanted you to come."

My brain was slow to process. "For taking the bar exam?"

"No. It's her birthday on Friday. How did you forget?"

Today was August seventeenth. *Shit.* "Man, I've been swamped. So, you want something on the actual day? The twentieth?"

"Yeah. I've already got her committed. She thinks she's coming for family dinner. But I figured you would come. Dustin. See whether your girls could come then some of Quinn's friends. She would appreciate it."

I got into my car and threw my briefcase into the passenger seat. My mind was spinning with guilt and excitement. Quinn's birthday. That was the night I'd planned to ask her to spend the night at my house. Being reminded it was her birthday was making my idea even more compelling. Not only would it be a special evening for her, but I wanted to make it a special night. She deserved something more than my cock, though.

A gift.

"Did I lose you?" Greg's voice brought me back to reality.

"Uh. No. Just pulling into traffic. That sounds like a great plan. And you said Quinn doesn't know, right?"

"Not a clue. She's been too busy starting this new journey with you that she's been in seventh heaven."

If he only knew... "Yeah. Okay. Text me the time, and I'll be there. I'll invite Cera and Christina, but don't hold your breath."

"Great. Also, thanks for taking Quinn under your wing. I'm a proud dad right now. My youngest will be a lawyer, and she'll be with the man I trust most in my life. You get it. From a dad's perspective, there's no one I'd rather her be learning from."

I swallowed the guilty memory of how sweet Quinn's pussy had tasted and how addicting the feeling of her against my tongue was that I couldn't wait to sink my cock into her tightness. "Thanks," I grumbled, and it sounded more like a question than accepting a compliment. "You would do the same for me, man." Although, he would never fuck my daughter.

"Gotta run."

"Later." I ended the phone call and steered my car straight to the mall. What could I get Quinn for her birthday? It had to be something thoughtful.

An hour later, I was back at my house with two wrapped gifts, both of which I couldn't wait to give her.

Me: *Want to spend the night this Friday? I want to taste more of that pussy of mine.*

Quinn: *Hell yeah. I like that it's 'your' pussy.*

Me: *Me too.*

Then I sent a devil emoji.

Quinn: *Tell me what you want to do to your pussy.*

Me: *Watch it squeeze my cock. Make it quiver from multiple orgasms. Feel it squirt all over my hand.*

Quinn: *That's dirty. But I love it. Friday works for me.*

Me: *Good. I can't wait to see you in your birthday suit. In my bed.*

Quinn: *LOL. You remembered it's my birthday Friday. How sweet.*

Me: *I even got you a present.*

Quinn: *You did?!?! What is it?*

Me: *I can't tell. You'll have to find out when you show up Friday night. A sure way to get you to my house.*

Quinn: *I'd come without the birthday present. I want to experience everything with you.*

Me: *No regrets about what we did in your office?*

Quinn: *Never! I hate that we got interrupted. It only made me want more. For you to unload inside me.*

Quinn: *I know you might think this is silly. I feel safe with you. I trust you.*

Me: *Are you on birth control?*

Quinn: *Yeah. Send me a picture. Please.*

This time, Q sent me purple heart emojis.

Me: *Of what?*

Quinn: *Well... I got to feel your hard cock, but I really want a picture of it.*

I couldn't do that. What if it spread all over the internet or she—

Quinn: *Stop thinking too much. I'm never sharing it with anyone. I really want to see what is mine.*

I laughed. I replayed the video she'd sent me last week, enough to get my dick hard, then I snapped a picture of my erection. Who was this man I was turning into?

I hit Send before I could think too much about it. It was scary and exhilarating. I was too old for this shit. But it was fun. And I knew it would make Quinn happy.

Quinn: *You're sexy. And big. Friday cannot come soon enough.*

She included an emoji of an eggplant, but I had zero clue what the fuck that was all about.

CERA AND CHRISTINA couldn't come to Quinn's party, which wasn't a big surprise. Holly had invited them to go with her and her new boyfriend. I was tired of feeling the pang in my heart every time Holly came to my mind. After all the time we'd been apart, it seemed like the pain should have passed. Maybe heartbreak stayed in the system.

I clutched the little gift bag and stepped up onto the porch. I was five minutes late, but when I opened the door,

Quinn's voice was unmistakable. Guilt pinged the backs of my eyelids, making my left eye twitch.

"I can't believe no one said anything," Quinn said. Her back was to me, but my body was still very in tune to how her presence demolished the pain Holly had left in my chest. She looked amazing.

Dustin stood in the kitchen, talking to one of Quinn's girlfriends. Greg walked toward me, a large smile on his face. He looked the same as he always did—in need of a haircut and tired, but happy.

I released a breath. *He doesn't know.*

"You're late." Greg lifted his glass of beer to me.

"Sorry. Couldn't be helped."

Quinn turned around when I spoke, and the smile that lit up her face did wild things to my heart. I squeezed the bag tighter, feeling somewhat self-conscious about the extravagant gift. "Quinn, happy birthday."

She went into my arms like she belonged in them, right there in front of everyone, and it took everything I had in me to not kiss her. Christ, even hugging her was taking everything in me to not make it appear like I knew the curves of her waist, the way she tasted between her legs, or how sensitive she was at the spot right below her ear.

"I'm so glad you made it tonight. Even if you are late." She winked at me. "What's this? Tiffany & Company? Wow, you went all out, Counselor. Or do you prefer if I call you *boss*?"

Oh, shit. My cock twitched at her sassy words. Greg handed me a glass of beer, which I greedily accepted, hoping it would mask my arousal.

"You don't have to call me 'boss.' Open it." I couldn't wait for her to see it.

"Yeah, Quinn, open it." Hannah stood next to Quinn, eyeing me up and down like she'd never seen me before.

"Hi, Hannah."

"Hello. That is so nice of you to get Quinn something so fancy."

"Yeah, Tiffany. Makes my bouquet of flowers look awful," Dustin said.

It might have the trademark logo, but honestly, it wasn't like it broke my wallet. "I've known Q along time." I shrugged. "Nothing but the best for her."

"And, Dustin, your flowers are amazing. I haven't gotten flowers from anyone in a really long time."

Quinn pulled out the square box and handed Hannah the empty bag. My gaze was laser-focused on Quinn. She was going to love this. She took off the lid and handed it to Hannah then popped open the jewelry box. Like I'd imagined, a smile shot across her face. Her head fell back, and laughter bubbled from her throat. "This is the cutest thing I've ever seen."

She pointed the box outward for Hannah and Greg to see the necklace.

"A gavel?" Hannah laughed. "A start to your new career."

"It's perfect. So thoughtful. I love how the head of the gavel is the teal color. Thank you, Jason." She flew back into my arms, squeezing me extra tightly.

My lips brushed against her ear. "It was either that or a paddle," I whispered.

Quinn stiffened in my arms. *Shit.* Had I gone too far?

She pulled back, a shy smile on her face. "I'll take both," she said. "Help me put this on."

She pulled the necklace free and handed me the chain while everyone else went back to their conversations, leaving Quinn and me in the living room. My fingers fumbled while undoing the clasp, and for some wild reason, my heart was soaring to new heights. If I wasn't careful, the entire room was going to know she was mine. It was so easy to touch her and tease her—I wasn't expecting that—especially in front of her father.

With the necklace on, Quinn turned to face me. "How do I look?"

She was so much younger than I was, but I swore she could see into my soul. Her eyes pierced mine and she gave me that rebel grin of hers.

"You look like a million bucks, Q."

Dinner was spaghetti, and Quinn popped garlic bread into the oven because Greg had no clue about the broil option. I sat across from Quinn at the dinner table. It was torture watching her lick her lips, acting all innocent when her foot was sliding up and down my leg. If she slid it high enough—I caught her ankle in my hand while Greg went on about all the ways listening to music had changed over time.

"What's your favorite song, birthday girl?" I asked, still holding her ankle. No one seemed to notice what was happening underneath the table.

I spread my legs and placed her foot on the edge of my chair. I scooted forward and pressed her foot into my crotch.

Her eyes widened. "Hmmm. So hard."

It sure was. The lighting hit her face perfectly. She stole my breath away.

"What's hard?" Greg asked.

I gripped her ankle, holding it in place when she tried to pull it away. "Ahh. Hard." She stuttered like she didn't know what the question was.

I chuckled. "I asked Q what her favorite song is."

She bit her lip, and her ankle pumped back and forth,

presumably in search of my cock again. "It's a hard choice. There are too many. I can't choose just one."

Contact. She slid her toes up my shaft the best she could.

"I agree with her. Tough choice." Greg stood, and Quinn moved her foot away from my crotch. "But speaking of songs, let's sing 'Happy Birthday.'"

Dustin helped Greg light candles, and Greg set the cake in front of her. Her eyes met mine. I mouthed the words of the song while she stared at me. Her eyes slowly moved around the group. I couldn't help but wonder what she was going to wish for. Right at the end, her eyes met mine again. She gave me her rebel look, and I knew her wish had something to do with me.

All night, my dick had been riding on the edge of going into full hard-on mode as I watched Quinn move around the kitchen, bending over in her short shorts, and a few times, she bent over in front of me, giving me a clear shot of her braless chest. Then at the table, it had been hard as hell.

I was a dead man tonight. I feared I would explode quicker than I wanted when it came time to have her in my bed.

"I'm heading out. Thanks for having me," I said to Greg. Quinn looked up from her conversation with Hannah. I mouthed, "Bye."

She walked toward Greg and me.

"Appreciate you coming over. We on for next month?" Greg asked. He and Quinn followed me to the front door.

I shouldn't. Not with the way I was letting his daughter touch my dick under his dinner table. Seriously, it was a sinful level to be at. But I was addicted. "I'll be here. Happy birthday." I gave Q a look, indicating that she'd better get her ass over to my house because I would be waiting. I wanted to sink into her body so fucking badly.

"I know I've told you a million times, but thank you for the necklace. It's beautiful." She fingered her necklace for the twentieth time this evening. "All right, Dad, let's clean up. I have somewhere to be."

I strolled to my car and adjusted my dick the second I slid into my seat. *What the fuck is wrong with me?* My nerves were fried like I'd never had sex before. The drive home was a blur because all I could think about was my other present for Quinn and how long it would take for her to show up.

Lucky for me, when I cracked open a beer, my phone lit up with a text from Quinn: *OMW*.

On my way. That short lingo, I was familiar with because of the girls. It took me three minutes of pacing before I said, "Fuck it," and went out into my garage. She had to park in here for the night. Minutes later, headlights blazed down my street. I released a deep breath, trying to calm myself down.

Quinn pulled into my driveway. I blinked against the glare, directing her to pull inside my garage. All the way in, she shut off her Jeep, and I closed the overhead door. She stepped out, her smile blazing about as brightly as her headlights.

She flew into my arms, and I picked her up, wrapping her legs around my waist. "It took me forever to leave. It was all I could do not to follow you out."

We made it inside, and I carried her down the hallway and straight to my bed. I loved how full of passion she was. She kissed me with her tongue and nibbled against my lips in between breaths. Her hands were wild through my hair, pulling me against her while her body climbed me like I was a tree.

She landed with a soft thud on my bed. Damn. I enjoyed this Quinn. Smart. Grown up. Gorgeous. Sinful.

She glanced around my room. "I've never been in here before. Now, when I think about you, I can think about you being in here and having a clear image of how it looks."

"Baby, from now on, you can come in here anytime you want." My cock was excruciatingly hard. This was finally going to happen.

"You're amazing. Thanks for making this the best birthday of my life."

I chuckled. "It's just getting started as far as I'm concerned." I kneeled in front of her and pulled off her shoes, trying to go slow and savor this first time with her. I kissed her calves, her knees, and up to her thighs, trying not to let my heart get swept up in this crazy sensation.

"What are you going to do to me?"

"There are a million things I want to do to you, but I'm not sure of your limits. For now, I'm going to go slow and hard. Give you all the filthy sex you've been missing."

Quinn sucked her bottom lip into her mouth. "I want it all. Everything."

I paused, enjoying her soft smooth skin beneath the pad of my thumb. "What is everything to you, Quinn?"

She writhed her body on the bed. Her fingers gripped the comforter. Her cheeks were pink. "Umm. I've never done anything with a guy except regular sex. And head. I've given head, but it was nothing like what Kimber was doing to you—"

"Quinn, let's not bring her up now, please." I didn't want this moment to be tainted or ruined in any capacity.

She giggled. "It's fine. I'm just telling you. So anyway, I

want it all. All the porn I've watched, I find myself very turned on by it all. The sex, of course."

"Of course."

"But the dirty talk. Being blindfolded. Spanked. Three-somes. How they use toys sometimes." She squeezed her thighs against my hands, which were still caressing her smooth skin. "All of it. Whatever. I'm down. And after walking in on you getting head, I know you're dirty, and I want it all with you." She looked away then back to me. "Except anal. I'm not sure I'd want that."

Anal? Christ, I haven't experienced that for twenty years when Holly and I were newly married, exploring one another and she figured out she didn't like it.

"Are one of those your biggest fantasies?"

I know she'd said it almost teasingly, but the truth was that my biggest fantasy was anal. It was the forbidden. The one thing I'd had just once with Holly. I'd watched it in plenty of porn videos—along with everything else that turned me on. And anal with Quinn? "I love everything you talked about, and I want it all... including anal. That's my fantasy."

"Oh. Of course. The one thing that doesn't appeal to me. I'm already starting out as a disappointment to you."

"Bullshit. If we never did it, I would be fine. I want you. That isn't a condition upon my wanting to be with you. What is it about it that doesn't appeal to you?"

She shrugged. "It's an exit, not an entrance. It doesn't seem very clean. And it sounds like it would hurt. Bad."

"I don't think it hurts when it's done right." At least that was what they portrayed in the movies. "Regardless, it's not something I expect, and if you ever trust me enough to want to do it, we can explore." I felt it was necessary to add, "But from here on out, you're mine, Q. And I'm going to give you everything you want."

I pulled her top off, exposing her tits. Her nipples were perfection, and I was in awe at the transformation from perfect room-temp studs to hard, perky nipples beneath the ceiling fan.

"Take this off. I have to feel you," she said.

I unbuckled my belt and pulled my shirt out of my pants. Unbuttoned it and enjoyed the sensation of Quinn rubbing her hands along my chest. An electric current zipped through my toes, legs, and arms and across my chest. Her hands traveled south to my zipper. "What are you gonna do, Q?"

Our eyes locked, and her signature look of smirk and naughty crossed her face. "Be the dirty girl you need me to be."

I groaned when her hand slid down my boxer briefs and stroked my dick. There was no way I could last as long as she deserved. Yeah, I jerked off all the freaking time, but it was nothing compared to being inside Quinn's tight heat.

I pulled her hand away. "I'll likely explode too soon if you continue to touch me like that."

"That's what I want." She licked her lips, her eyes glued to my cock. "For you to lose control."

I chuckled. "Oh, I will. Just not our first time." I pushed her back and grazed my mouth along the skin of her neck. "I'm gonna make you come so hard, Quinn. My bed is going to be soaked when we're done."

Much like I had in her office, I went down on her. She was freaking amazing. Everything I wanted in a partner—passionate, horny, dirty, not to mention intelligent—Quinn was it. My hair burned from her trying to pull me away and yet pushing my face tight against her while I fucked her with my mouth. That—the tonguing her pussy—I could do. I was an expert at oral.

I could do it all fucking night. Talk about a power trip. I could tease and taunt her with my mouth. She was mine. I owned her tonight. I was in charge down here and on top of the world with a beautiful young woman at my mercy. I slid my fingers inside her, loving the way she clamped down against my knuckles. How could something so forbidden feel so right? I pushed the thoughts away that tried to invade my mind about all the reasons I shouldn't be doing this to her.

"Yes. Right there. Jason. I'm going to come."

Quinn's entire body went tight, and I gave her all I could to carry her over the edge.

"You can do that to me anytime you want."

I smiled at the sound of her spent voice. I kissed her all the way up her stomach, placed quick kisses on her breasts—*I'll come back to you two*—and licked a trail up her neck, stopping so we were face-to-face. "I love how alive and passionate you are in my hands. What do you want next?" I teased, even though I was really hoping she was going to say sex.

She nipped at my lips. "I've always wanted to taste myself against a guy's skin." She swirled her tongue along my bottom lip. "That day at your office was surreal."

I wrapped my hand beneath her neck and pushed my tongue over hers. Her hands locked on to my shoulders, and she met the motions of my mouth thrust for thrust.

Quinn pulled back. "I taste good on your lips."

I chuckled. "Yeah, you do."

Her fingers moved across my lips, and I used the minutes to stare into her eyes. They were dazzling, happy, and breathtaking. She raised her hips, pushing herself against my dick. "This line can't be uncrossed, Quinn. You sure about going forward?"

She blew a breath across my jaw. "I've never wanted anyone like this before. It's a scary feeling, honestly."

Yeah, it was. "It means a lot to me to hear you say how much you trust me and want to experience all this sexual stuff with me. And not just some young, dumb kid who can't appreciate you and give you what you need."

"You're definitely the man for the job."

My cock twitched. "Damn right I am." I pressed the head of my dick against her entrance. It took all my willpower to take it slow. This was monumental.

"You feel better than I imagined."

"You think you can handle me?" I winked and pushed forward, not inside her but enough that my dick was against her slickness, ready to probe.

Her breath hitched. She was a little nervous but typical Quinn, I could tell by the look on her face, she was going to power through it. "I'm going to handle you so well you won't want to go anywhere else. Ever."

I pushed slowly inside her, clenching my eyes shut because she was tight, and it'd been too long for me. And I feared that Quinn's promise of *handling me so well* was the truth.

9

QUINN

Jason swallowed my gasp with his mouth. I talked a good deal of crap, but truthfully, I wasn't prepared for him. He stretched me painfully well, and as if he knew I needed time to adjust, he pulled out and entered me again slowly. His tongue mimicked his movements, and I could hardly think beyond it gliding smoothly over my tongue. How was I going to make Jason feel as amazing as he was making me feel?

"Quinn, are you uncomfortable?"

"No."

"Do you want me to stop?"

"No."

"Why are you thinking so hard? Why are you so tense?" His lips brushed against mine, and I realized he was absolutely right.

I sucked in a deep breath and released it, feeling my body loosen. "I was trying to figure out how I was going to make you as happy as you've been making me."

He chuckled against my cheek. His warm breath sent the good shivers down my spine. I clenched against him.

"Already one step ahead? How about you relax and stay in the moment with me?"

I shifted beneath his weight and wrapped my legs around him, causing him to push deeper into me. "I'm in the moment now. Is this good for you?"

He pressed up onto his arms, and I looked into his eyes —really looked into them. My heart fluttered. It was hard to decipher what he was thinking, but he was the man who could give me everything I craved.

He placed a quick, light kiss on my mouth. "Your pleasure is my pleasure. So, fuck yeah, it's good for me."

He started moving his hips again. With each flex and pull, my worries vanished. The pleasure was a slow burn because that was the pace Jason kept. Was he worried he would come too quickly?

"Faster."

He let out a groan and lifted back, holding my legs up into a V so I was fully exposed to him. I took in the beautiful sight of him moving into me. The way I was stretched around him. How muscular he was. All his chest hair, which when the light hit him perfectly, was mostly gray and yet still sexy as hell.

"What do you need, Q? I'm not going to last. It's been too long."

What do I need? I was taken aback by such a thoughtful question. No one I'd ever had sex with had asked or cared. "I want to come again."

"Touch yourself."

His order made my heart skip. I liked how bossy he sounded. My fingers found my center, and it was thrilling that I was touching myself while he was thrusting in and out of me. I couldn't seem to get over my stage fright, though, rubbing one way, not getting in sync with myself.

"Do it the way you always do. The way you know you'll get off."

His fingers gripped my calves, and I found my rhythm, rubbing myself while Jason fucked me. His face was set in grim determination. His eyes were glued to mine, and even though he'd said it earlier, in that moment, it sunk in. My pleasure was his pleasure. Suddenly, it wasn't all that bad that I was lying on his mattress spread apart and massaging my clit while he watched.

With my free hand, I pinched my nipples one at a time like I did when I was alone, and with him already inside me, I found my rhythm.

"Atta girl. Come for me, babe."

It was the guttural sound out of Jason's throat that sent me over the edge. My orgasm sent shockwaves through my entire body. I tried hard to keep my eyes open because I was desperate to watch Jason lose his cool. To see him at his weakest. He tipped his head back and stilled his movements. Warm liquid filled me.

My heart settled down. I was confident this man would give me what I needed and that I could be good for him in return. Him coming inside of me was more than having sex without a condom. It broke a barrier. He trusted me. I trusted him. A possessiveness I'd never experienced settled over me. He practically collapsed onto me in a heap of sweat and post-arousal.

"Fucking hell, Q. I already want more of you," he said into the curve of my neck.

I loved the way he smelled. I loved how I'd made him feel this way. "Well, it's a good thing we have all night, then."

He raised his head and looked me directly in the eyes. "Tonight is you and me, together. No kink. Not tonight."

He kissed my nose. "Well, maybe something small if you're a good girl."

A thrill shot through me. "I can be a good girl. I can be a bad girl too. Whatever you want."

"Putting me in charge, huh?"

"At least until I build some confidence. Then I'll be the one in control." I was completely okay with following Jason's lead and doing whatever he wanted. I knew he would lead me well. I didn't have anything to be scared about.

"Oh, Q." He sucked my bottom lip into his mouth and released it on a pop. "You have more control over me than you think." His hands went to my necklace, and I craned my neck to see what he was doing. His fingers toyed with the pendant.

"Hey, I thought you said you had another present for me?" I asked.

Jason rolled off me, and I scooted over on the bed to make room for him. It was the best sex I'd ever had. *How is my future life without this ever going to match this? Be better than this?*

"Do you want to open it now?"

"Of course! You can't tease me all night."

He rose onto his elbow and faced me. His mouth curved into a coy little grin. I touched one of his dimples with my fingertip.

"I can. And I will. But your present is also a present for me, so without further ado... I'll be right back." He rolled off the bed and padded down the hallway.

Anxious and excited, I stood and followed him. By the time I made my way down the hall and into his kitchen, he was bending over the back of his couch, presumably retrieving my gift.

But the view? I held my breath, taking in all the angles and curves of him. Dark hair covered his thighs, up to the apex of his legs, where the hottest view I'd ever seen in my freaking life dangled to perfection. I remembered I wasn't breathing and sucked in a deep breath.

Jason was my fantasy.

"Enjoying the view?"

My eyes moved up, and that was when I saw he was watching my reflection in his living room window. Thankfully, his house butted up to a wildlife preserve, and the neighbors he did have were at least a house apart from each other.

My cheeks warmed. "I'd be a fool not to. I've never seen anything so amazing in my life." It was God's honest truth, and I wanted him to know.

With my eyes still glued on the window, he walked toward me, holding my gift in his hands. It was small like my Tiffany box but didn't have a discernable branding to it. He touched my arm with the gift, and I turned to face him. "I like how uninhibited you are."

I glanced down at my naked body. "I feel safe with you. Nothing to be ashamed of."

His eyes traveled down my body, from top to bottom. "Hell no, there isn't. Open it."

I took the box, and my heart thumped heavily. My stomach tightened against all the whirling inside it. This present was going to be more personal. More meaningful. Though the gavel was pretty meaningful itself, this one was going to be different. "I'm nervous." My fingers trembled as I fumbled with the lid.

"Don't be."

The lid popped off and fell to the floor, but Jason

pushed on my arm when I went to retrieve it. "Okay." I pulled the tissue away and gasped. "This is beautiful."

I pulled out the fabric—a blindfold—and a little gift card tumbled out from the cloth. I saw what the gift card was for, but I was too transfixed.

"Is it okay?"

I glanced up at the weariness in Jason's voice. "Yeah. I told you I wanted this." I let the satin fabric slip through my fingers. The purple was majestic threaded with the black. "It's gorgeous. Where did you find something like this?"

Jason shrugged like it was no big deal. "The store."

"And the gift card? For ice cream? We should totally order some now." I held the card in my other hand, still enthralled with the sexy garment. "Put it on me. Just for a second. Like a pretest."

Jason's chuckle vibrated from his throat, a mix of a growl and laughter. "Turn around. Tell me when you want it off. If it makes you nervous or anything. Promise?"

"Of course. Sure." I let it slip from my hands and turned around like I had done with my necklace earlier. I closed my eyes.

The warmth of Jason's body against mine was exquisite. He was warm and hard, and when the satiny fabric slipped over my eyes, blocking out the light, my desire quickly escalated.

"Hold still," Jason said against my hair.

My shoulders relaxed. The first tie drew my skin taught along my forehead. "I feel so... so sexy," I said breathlessly.

"You look stunning."

"I haven't turned around."

"I'm watching you in the window." The second knot tightened. Jason's hands were on my shoulders. "You good?"

I smiled, allowing my body the freedom to truly feel what was happening. "Yeah. Just don't move for a second."

His hands were rough. Calluses. His cock was heavy against my lower back, soft like the satin but so rigid. Our bodies weren't breathing in sync. His breaths were long and slow. Mine were short and fast. "This is amazing."

I heard him smile. Or maybe I felt it. If I were to take off the blindfold, his dimples would be showing.

"What are you experiencing?"

I swallowed. "You."

"What about me?" His voice was amazing. Low, like the rumble of a sports car. Seductive. It had a little twang to it that I'd never noticed before.

"You have calluses even though you work at a desk."

"From lifting weights."

"You're extremely hard right now. But your skin is so soft."

His breath tickled my ear. "'Cause you're beautiful."

"And you're so calm."

He turned me around slowly so I was facing him. He never took a hand off me, but he reached for mine and lifted it. He pulled my fingers apart. "Make them flat."

I stretched my hand like I was going to give him a high five.

He placed it over his chest. Despite his calm breaths, his heart was beating fast. "I don't feel calm. I feel like every nerve in my body has come to life. I feel like I might explode with feelings I've never had before. I feel like I'm brand-new, experiencing this world with a different set of eyes."

"Because of what we're doing?"

"Because of you, Quinn."

He untied the blindfold, and I caught it in my hands. I blinked a few times, getting my eyes to adjust. I turned around to Jason and pulled him to me. "This is the best birthday I've had. Like ever."

He wrapped his arms around me. "Like ever?" he teased. "What about that time your mom and dad surprised you with tickets to see Taylor Swift? I thought that was your best birthday ever."

"Oh my gosh. That was the first—well, the only—time I'd ever been in a limo."

Jason released me. "And remember the driver went down the wrong one way, and all those cars were honking at us?"

I laughed. "I was sure we were all going to die. Cera was on the verge of tears."

Jason laughed. "She is so dramatic sometimes. I'm sorry I couldn't get her to come tonight."

I shook my head. "You're enough. Honestly, I like Cera, but I'm glad she wasn't there. I like having you all to myself." *That was a good birthday, but this one...* "This birthday is topping that one by far, just so you know."

"I hope so."

Jason kissed me, and I was floored with how right this felt. It was crazy. He was twenty years older than me, but it didn't feel like that. He was a normal guy. If I didn't know his age in numbers, I wouldn't know. "Hey. Let's have some ice cream delivered. They're open all night. It's one of their specialties."

"I saw that when I picked up your gift card. Some desperate people out there for them to be open all night with delivery."

"Ice cream makes people do crazy things. It's addicting. Trust me, I would know. I eat it every day."

"What are you going to get?"

"A variety." I shrugged. "I'll ask for a surprise. Then we can taste test." I held up my blindfold. "With my new gift."

I loved making Jason laugh. And once we'd agreed on ice cream flavors neither of us cared for so they didn't wind up in our surprise flavor pack, we placed an order and got dressed. It was already approaching midnight, but I was wide awake. I used his bathroom, fixed my smeared eye makeup, and met Jason in the living room. He was shirtless, wearing gray sweatpants that rode along his hips.

"Is it going to be weird working together?"

He patted the couch next to him, and I took a seat. "No. Only the fact that I'm going to want to touch you every fucking second you're around me."

I leaned back along the armrest, and he pulled my feet into his lap. He began making lazy circles with his fingertips. He adjusted my toe ring so the heart was facing the sky. He tapped the five freckles on the top of my left foot. He was calm and quiet. His brow furrowed in concentration while he connected an imaginary line from freckle to freckle. I could watch him all night. He was intriguing. Sexy. My body yearned to soak up as much of him as I could in the small amount of time we would have. This wasn't forever.

"We'll have to be careful around everyone." That was not going to be easy after tonight. It was as if Jason was already all mine. I wanted the world to see. "I know you already know that... but I already feel like I have rights to you."

Jason glanced up from my feet. He stared at me for a long while but didn't say anything. I shouldn't have said what I did. But it was the truth. And it wasn't like he was some dumb college guy who would immediately think I was getting attached anyway.

The doorbell cut through the silence, and we both got to our feet. "I'll get it."

"No. I'll get it. Stay put." The vehemence in his voice reminded me of why I couldn't get it. The feeling didn't settle well.

"Fine. Here's my card." I handed him the gift card.

He gave me a little smirk. "Seems weird to use this on me when I got it for you."

"I think you had an ulterior motive."

"I think I can't wait to cover your tits in ice cream."

The comment shot thrills through me. Jason answered the door and paid, and I gazed around the room, appreciating his house from a new viewpoint. I was no longer Quinn the family friend. I was Quinn the family friend with benefits.

The door squeaked shut, and Jason brought our box of ice cream to the kitchen. "There's no way we're eating all this tonight."

"Is the box full?"

Jason took off the lid and withdrew a few bags of ice packs.

I counted quickly. "Eight cartons. They're small, though."

"Small? Q, they're just like the Ben and Jerry's cartons at the store. One of these cartons can be for two people."

I bit my lip. "You've never seen me eat ice cream." I nudged him aside, thinking of how we were going to do this. But there was only one way. "Here. I'll take four, and you take four. I get to blindfold you first."

"Don't peek at the other ones."

"I would never. Here. Close your eyes." I closed my eyes so I wouldn't accidentally see what the other ones were and grabbed two cartons, set them behind the box out of

Jason's line of vision, then got two more. I put the ice packs back inside and put the lid on.

"Open." I picked up my blindfold and made a twirling motion with my fingers. "No. Wait. Can't we be naked? It will be more fun that way."

Jason laughed but didn't even hesitate to push his sweats down his lean legs. He stepped out of them, and I followed suit.

"Now turn." Jason turned around. Was the blindfold going to be the same way for him as it was for me? I slid it over his face and tied it, giving him a second to adjust to the darkness while I stepped back and admired him. My hand trailed over his shoulder and across his shoulder blade. I went down his spine, loving the ridges and curves of his muscles. He had muscles everywhere. My hands flitted to his ass.

"Grab it." His voice was quiet. Something about the blindfold made everything mysterious and quiet. It was like we were edging on the dark side and didn't want to be too loud for fear of breaking it.

His ass cheeks. He wanted me to squeeze them. But I had different ideas.

I reached around him and grabbed his cock, loving how erect and thick it was in the palm of my hand. I gave a slow stroke, letting him savior the sensitized feeling of being blindfolded.

My body pressed against his back, and I reached around with my other hand. His balls were large. Tight. Firm. I gently bit the skin of his shoulder, loving the low grunt that escaped his mouth.

"How is this?" I massaged his balls and stroked him slowly.

"Much better than doing it myself."

He tilted his head into me as best he could. I understood completely what he meant. I released him and stepped back. His hand went to the counter to steady himself.

"Our ice cream will melt." I opened the first lid. "Spoons?"

"Top drawer to the left of the fridge."

I grabbed two and dipped his into the first carton. Chocolate Cherry Love. "Turn around."

The second he turned to me, my heart leapt into my throat. The blindfold added this mysterious layer of provocativeness to him. It also made me feel powerful, like I had this control over his actions. It gave me confidence and strength, like I could stand up to any person I needed to and exert a sense of confidence I didn't normally feel like I had.

"Open your mouth." Oh, now that was sexier. "I should take a picture of you like this."

His lips quirked into a smile. "Why?"

"I've never witnessed anything so sexy." Then I realized I just had. "Well, except for the way you were bent over the couch. But this is a different kind of sexy."

I tentatively touched his lips with the spoon. His tongue swiped the first drops of ice cream.

"I'm sticking it in your mouth now."

"That's supposed to be my line," he teased. He held the ice cream in his mouth then worked his jaw before swallowing. "Definitely chocolate."

I nodded. "What else?"

"Raspberry or Cherry. It's fruity for sure."

"Good guesses. That one was Chocolate Cherry Love. Next up." I opened the next carton and dipped the spoon. This was some kind of Butter Brickle Bonanza. New to me. "Open wide."

He swiped the ice cream off the spoon quickly and chewed. He hadn't even swallowed it before he guessed. "Butter Brickle. My favorite."

"Never heard of it. But you're right."

Jason raised his shoulders. "How have you never heard of Butter Brickle? It's a classic."

"That explains it. Anytime someone uses the word *classic*, that means it's old. This is an old person's ice cream."

I loved how the blindfold bunched up on his face when he smiled. "You're right—it is. Was my grandfather's favorite."

My grandfather preferred apple pie and vanilla ice cream. So basic. "Next one." This one was Key Lime Pie, which sounded good to me.

He opened his mouth. The ice cream dripped onto his lips, and I laughed while he closed his mouth around the spoon. My cheeks hurt from smiling. If someone cut my heart open right now, it would explode with confetti.

I leaned forward, put my hands on his forearms, and kissed off the key lime ice cream. He let out a little groan. His five-o'clock shadow was bristly against my chin. The ice cream tasted superb—better coming from his lips.

"I could get used to this," he said.

He took control then. His hand cupped the back of my head, and his lips ravished me. I moaned into his mouth when his tongue slid along the seam of my lips then over my tongue. A mixture of key lime and graham cracker tinged my taste buds.

The spoon clattered to the tile floor. His hands roamed down the sides of my body to cup my ass. I loved this so much. The way he dominated me. His confidence. The way he was so interested in me. Touching me. Feeling me.

Devouring me. It was like I was the only thing that mattered to him. *How have I dated guys who were never into me like this?*

"There's one more flavor for you to try," I murmured against his lips.

"Rub it on your nipples." He released me. "Sit up here on the counter."

I pushed a few cartons and the box aside, and he helped me up. I opened the last carton and dipped the spoon. It was aptly named Party Time—vanilla with sprinkles. Basic. "It's going to melt the instant I put it on my nipples."

"Don't worry. I'm going to lick every last drop of it off you."

"Be ready," I warned. I dropped the ice cream onto my nipple, where it slipped around, already traveling down the curve of my breast. "Hurry!"

I laughed and guided his head to my nipple. He took me into his mouth, making exaggerated sounds like he was tearing me apart.

"You're tickling me."

His mouth coasted down the curve of my breast, following the trail. He hooked his arms beneath my legs, spreading me apart. It was a turn of events for sure.

"Shouldn't I be wearing the blindfold for this?" I asked when his tongue licked most of the path clean. The original scoop settled into the curve of my thigh, dripping to the inside and outside of my thigh.

"Nope. This is my turn, and you taste fucking glorious."

"You haven't even guessed what flavor it is."

He paused and raised his face. "Vanilla with sprinkles. I inhaled two back up at mile marker breast zone."

"Technically, it's called Party Time."

"You're telling me I can finally use the line, 'There's a

party in my mouth; wanna come?'" He nibbled the skin along my tummy, tickling me.

"Ha ha. Yes. That line works surprisingly well right now. And the answer is yes, yes I fucking do."

Jason's mouth reached the crease of my thigh, where he licked what he could find before his mouth was on my clitoris, sucking and licking me for all he was worth. He slid his fingers inside me, and it didn't take me long before I was lying flat on my back, screaming his name while wave after wave of pleasure shot through me.

I undid the blindfold in a hurry because I was dying to see his eyes. I grabbed a dishtowel and folded it along the floor near his feet. "It's about time I get to do this."

I kneeled in front of him, just the way I'd played over and over in my imagination. Jason's muscles were tight. The muscles along his forearms flexed. I got to my knees. It was hard to read the look in his eyes. He didn't give much away. But the power in the air was making me dizzy.

I stroked him. I put my lips to his head and gave a long, slow swipe. He leaned back against the counter, but he didn't take his eyes off me, and I didn't want him to. In fact, I wanted to do this and look up at him. But I couldn't do both. Not if I wanted to do it well.

I looked up at him one last time while he pressed his cock slowly into my mouth. His girth stretched my jaw and lips tight. His hips pressed forward. *Fucking fuck.*

I thought this was supposed to make him lose control, but there I was, somehow being brought to the ledge of pure ecstasy again. My pussy clenched, squeezing itself, merely being caressed by air while his cock plunged in and out of my throat.

Jason's hand went to my neck. He gripped me tightly, withdrawing his cock, then plunging it back inside.

If I didn't get this under control, I was going to come. *Oh fuck. It's happening.* I closed my eyes, giving in to the sensation of how amazing he felt inside of my mouth and how hungry for him I actually was. How powerless.

"Are you coming, little girl?"

My knees throbbed, threatening to buckle. My entire body shook.

"Answer me." He thrust inside me faster, deeper. Harder. "I want to know that my cock in your mouth is enough to make you come."

I nodded, his cock restricting me from moving my head too much. I clenched my eyes closed. The sensation was too much to handle. *How am I not biting off his dick?*

"Open your eyes, Q."

I pried them apart, my clit flying off the rails of the strongest orgasm I'd had yet tonight. My neck fell back, and he took the opportunity to thrust his dick as far into my mouth and throat as it would go.

"That's a good girl. Swallow everything I give you."

I had no other thoughts. I couldn't agree vocally, but I welcomed it. I wanted this. I wanted him. He emptied himself inside my mouth. His eyes closed.

"Fuck." He growled and released his grip on my neck while I sucked him as well as I could considering I was about to go jelly. His mouth quirked into one of his sexy grins that showcased his dimples, and he met my gaze. This was what I've wanted since that night—Jason powerless. Or was it me who was powerless and under his control?

He pulled out of my mouth, and when he helped me stand, he brushed his thumb underneath my eye. "I've ruined your makeup."

You've ruined more than my makeup. I was never going to be the same after that.

10

JASON

I opened my eyes slowly, fearing that if I opened them too quickly, the events from last night would mark themselves as a dream. But the tiny weight of Quinn's arm swung across my stomach was evidence that it hadn't been.

I was living on the line of heaven with my best friend's daughter, but at any moment, I could fall into the depths of hell. Enjoying something so fucking wonderful that I was beginning to believe that I deserved this small slice of heaven. I was a good man. I had been a good husband. I was a good dad. In all aspects of my life, I strived to be the bigger man, to do the better things. To be better.

This one small thing that I was indulging in couldn't be all that bad.

She slept on her stomach. At some point in the early morning hours, we'd kicked off the sheets. We both lay naked without covers. Didn't I deserve this? After all the wonderful things I'd done in my life—the good guy I had always been—if no one ever found out about this, we couldn't hurt anyone.

It was funny how the woman most off-limits to me was

the woman I'd had the best sex with in my entire life. Including my wife. How was that possible? Was it because it was forbidden? Because I knew it couldn't last forever? The connection we'd shared last night was astounding, to say the least.

My jaw ached. My chest was so full of love. Happiness. It was weird to recall how happy I'd been with Holly and the girls, but spending time like this with Quinn was true happiness. My bones had never felt this good. I looked forward to our days together. I looked forward to seeing her in the office. It was a wonderful change of pace to have something worth living for. I turned sideways so I was facing Quinn. It was five in the morning, and I had absolutely nowhere to be. I trailed my fingertips along her shoulder blades. She was thin. Her bones protruded from her shoulders and spine. Even her hips were jutted out, but her butt was round and firm. Small. I moved her arm and kneeled over her.

My lips met the sweetness of her skin along her lower back. "Are you ready for more?" I mumbled against her skin, traveling south to the sweet swells of her butt cheeks. I left a wet trail down one side and up the other.

She squirmed beneath my touch and mumbled, "That feels good."

I grabbed a pillow. "Lift your hips." I shoved the pillow beneath her stomach, propping her up enough so I could taste her sweet pussy.

I wet my fingers to push inside of her but found she was already wet for me. I made love to her pussy and her ass with my mouth and fingers, loving how her thighs quivered when she came. I wasn't ready to breach her virgin backside with my fingers, but I loved the way she puckered when I touched her there.

"Get on your knees, Quinn. This is your wake-up call."

"Will you wake me up like this every day?" Her voice was sleepy but breathless, and I found it utterly adorable. She complied with my wishes, and at her entrance I wet the head of my cock with her juices, sliding up and down a few times. I entered her slowly, knowing she was going to be tight. *But fuck me.*

"Don't move," I said. She had a choke hold on my dick, and the feeling was so intense, I was going to explode.

"Don't do this?" She wiggled her ass around.

My fingers dug into her hips, stopping her from moving. "Exactly."

"No. Let me do the work."

"You gonna stroke me off like this?"

She tipped her chin over her shoulder, pinning her eyes on me. She rolled her hips back and forth. "Is it gonna work?"

I couldn't answer as she began to move, taking me in long, slow thrusts. It was like she was giving me a lap dance, except I was inside of her. She must be a good dancer. How else could I explain this trick of the way she moved her hips in rotation? The way she slid up and down was magical—a magical vise that had me fucking mesmerized.

It took all my control to allow her to move this way instead of plunging into her and fucking her like the wild beast I was becoming. My balls tightened. My release was moving up my shaft, and after two more of her rotations, I was filling her. My toes curled. My chest tightened. My mind was hazy while I enjoyed my bliss.

"You like those moves?"

I pressed into her once more before I slid out. "God, yes. Were you a dancer in your previous life?"

Quinn turned around and lay flat on her back, that big

grin on her face like she was so proud of herself. "No. It just came to me. I did what I thought you would like."

"You watched it on porn, didn't you?"

She laughed, and red rose along her cheeks. "That obvious?"

I grabbed a towel and cleaned us both up as best as I could. "Not that obvious. I reached for the extreme because that seems to be you. And lo and behold, I was right." I slid next to her in my bed, wrapping my arm beneath her neck, pulling her into me. "I'm not complaining. Keep watching them to learn tricks to perform on me."

She was silent for a second, running her hand through my chest hair. "Maybe we could watch them together."

I glanced down at the top of her head. She was nervous at the suggestion. Who had she ever dated that was so judgmental of her desires? *Young fuckheads. That's who.* I envisioned Quinn and me watching porn together and how hot it would be. "That would be sexy as hell, wouldn't it? We could reenact everything."

She shifted and glanced up at me. "Yes, Counselor. It sure would."

We stayed quiet for a little while longer, and by Quinn's even breathing, I knew she had fallen back to sleep. I didn't move, but after years of waking up early, I wouldn't be able to fall back to sleep. And what I was experiencing was so tangled up in my mind, the truth was, I didn't know where to go from here. I hadn't had a lot of girlfriends since Holly. It wasn't like I'd ever dated in secret. I didn't know what to do next. Part of me wanted to call Greg and let him know I was sleeping with his twenty-six-year-old daughter and call it a day. The other part of me was scared to death that if I did that, this would end.

That thought had been prominent all night long, riding

along the throes of passion. This was a forbidden love affair that could never see daylight. I was a good man. But I was also a lonesome man.

And right now, my need for all this woman was offering me in secret was stronger than the best friendship I'd ever had. Stronger than my career and the possibility of this relationship losing the respect of my colleagues.

And that said a lot about my character and what kind of *good man* I actually was.

ONE THING I hadn't anticipated was how fucking hard it was to actually work with Quinn. All I could think about was my cock balls deep inside her pussy and her mouth. She was the utmost professional, no question. But boy, did she try my patience. Question after question about every single thing I did. Why do I do it this way and not this way? Why did I speak like that to people? Why didn't I have more pro bono cases? Why didn't I call it a day at five o'clock like all the other professionals?

"I'm telling you, Jason. This is how it should be. You're wasting my time. It takes me less time to scan all of these documents than it does for me to go through them all individually and put them in the order you're wanting."

I blew out a breath. I hadn't anticipated the weight of how much digital technology had influenced Quinn's life, personal and professional. A digital calendar we could share? I trusted technology to pay my bills, but I didn't trust it enough to rely on it for all of my appointments. "Quinn. Please, go through them. I don't have the time to reassess this now. Plus, I like hard copies."

"Hard copies are outdated—they have secure email

now. They have password thingies that you can send people, and they have to have the passcode to open the email. How do you not know all of this already?" She looked up at me beneath her glasses.

She was wearing a white blouse today that had buttons down the front. I'd let her start wearing jeans on the days I didn't have court and she wasn't assisting me with clients in my office. The joke was on me, though, because I preferred her tight ass in the jeans more than I did in those pencil skirts she wore. It was embarrassing how many times I'd caught myself watching her move around wearing those fucking jeans.

I leaned forward. My mouth was inches from hers. "Have you ever been spanked, Quinn? Because you're undermining my authority, and I have every bit the urge to bend you over my knee and spank the fuck out of you right now."

Her face flushed scarlet, and for a second she stared at me like I'd slapped her, but then her eyes got that look in them—the look that was starting to make an appearance in my dreams. Not her rebel look, but her I-want-to-be-fucked-by-you-so-bad look. It slowly morphed into her rebel look. "We're working right now. You can't do that."

I raised my brow. I owned this fucking place. "Can't or won't? Stand up."

What the fuck am I doing? This was a sure-fire way to get caught by my receptionist or Salazar. I took Quinn's hand in mine and led her to my bookshelf. Her eyes were wide with desire, and my cock was a freaking flagpole of anticipation.

"Bend over. Right here." I pointed to my ladder. I would have preferred to slap her bare ass, but since we were both new at this, just one spank through her jeans was going to have to be okay for the both of us. I wished she were wearing a dress, though.

Quinn followed my instructions and braced both hands along the railings. I flicked the brakes down with the toe of my shoe. On second thought, thank God she wasn't wearing a dress because I would literally be inside her right now.

"You know what you're getting spanked for?"

She squeezed the railing and leaned forward so her breasts were touching the rungs. "For having better, more efficient ideas than you?"

I chuckled. God, she was sassy. And she was probably right, but I was in charge, and this was what the boss wanted. "You might earn yourself two spankings with that sarcastic mouth of yours."

I rubbed her butt with my hand, and the memories of Friday with her in my arms came flooding back—as if the memories had gone too far. "I'm spanking you because when we're in the office, I'm in charge and you shouldn't question my choices like I don't know what I'm doing. I've been doing this for twenty years. My system works."

"Your system could be better."

Thwap!

She let out a low moan. My hand stung. It wasn't super hard, but enough to jolt her forward. Her knuckles were white gripping the edges of the ladder. I cocked my head to the side. She'd come when she gave me a blow job. "Could you come like this, Q?"

She tried to speak, but only a squeak came out. She tried again. "I'm freaking horny enough that it couldn't possibly take much."

I began caressing her ass again. When had I turned into this man? I was in a shell of a man that didn't *seem* like me, but the heart of this guy was me. I was in an element, and only Quinn seemed to bring it out of me.

"You want me to spank you again?" I let my hand slip between the crease of her jeans to cover her mound.

"Do I deserve another spanking?"

I smiled. She was totally into this. "Well, you undermined my authority not once, but twice. Will you have learned your lesson after this?" I leaned forward, over her, so my lips were along the side of her neck. My dick was pressed tight against her ass. "What's it feel like? I want to know if you're going to come."

She let out a slow breath. "Honestly, yeah. I feel so close. I'm soaked right now."

I stood, stroking Quinn's back, down to her ass, where I started caressing it again. Caressing between her legs, I wished like hell I could feel her wetness coat my fingers. "What's it gonna take, Q? Another spanking?"

"Please. Fuck, yes. Please."

Thwap!

She jolted forward, and a low moan escaped her mouth. But I knew she wasn't having an orgasm. Yet. "Touch me. Help me. It's so close," she whined.

I slipped my hand between her legs, giving her what she demanded. One. Two. Three. Four. Five. Si—she started breaking apart against my hands.

"Oh, my gosh. I'm falling." Her knees buckled.

"I got you, baby." I pressed against her, not letting her fall, wanting her to enjoy the last remnants of her orgasm. She was putty in my hands, but it was weird because I was putty in her hands. Christ, I was at my office.

I helped her stand.

Back to work.

"When I mentioned being able to enjoy this ladder, I hadn't thought of using it quite like that."

I gave her a light smile. "It's versatile. Did I hurt you?"

Quinn laughed. "Gosh, no. It was... strangely good. I'll have to keep undermining your authority if that's my punishment every time."

I shook my head. "Next time, I won't be so nice. I won't let you come."

She stuck her lower lip out into a pout. "Maybe next time it will be me doing the spanking."

Deep laughter bubbled up from my throat. "I don't think so. But I would let you suck my balls."

Quinn pursed her lips. "Well, if you behave at work this week, I *would* let you fuck my ass." She turned on her heel, went straight to my door, and walked across the hallway to her office, closing the door with a light click.

Quinn's ass. Just when I felt like I was in control, it was her who was controlling me. My phone rang. Dustin. I hadn't seen him since the last party at Greg's, which was odd, but I'd been too wrapped up with Quinn to notice.

"Dude. Long time. What are you doing?" I asked.

"Oh, man. I've been busy as hell. We got a new contract." Dustin ran a concrete company that specialized in large commercial projects. No small time for this guy.

"That's good news. But I swear that happens to you at least once a month."

"Yeah." He coughed then asked, "How are you holding on?"

I glanced around my office, where piles of files lay strategically placed—all the files I'd been making Quinn go through for me. "Fine. Got Quinn here now. Helping."

Dustin laughed like he knew what kind of train wreck that might be. "Has she rearranged your office yet?"

"Not yet. Not for lack of trying. She's trying to get me to change up how I do things. Thinks paper is so old-fashioned. And less paper being printed would mean I'm helping the environment."

"What is it with this younger generation and technology? I sure as hell am not depending on any computer to run my life. Not to mention the fact that the way my luck goes, some cybercriminal would steal my shit and sell it to Russia."

"Right? Just an easy way for the government to keep closer tabs on us."

"Fuck that."

"Exactly." I didn't mention that I wasn't entirely opposed to Q's idea. I just didn't have the time right now to deal with it. "I'll be in court the next three days, so it is nice to have her help."

"Yeah, she'll learn a lot from you."

The image of Quinn bent over my ladder getting spanked flooded my mind. As did the image of her wearing her blindfold even though we had yet to use it during intercourse. "We're learning a lot from each other." That was the truth.

"That's great. I'm sure Greg is grateful to have you there for her."

"Uh, yeah. He is."

"You in the mood to go on a double date this weekend with Bonnie and her sister Silvie?"

My phone buzzed. Once. Twice. *A date? What about Quinn?* I almost said as much before I caught myself. "I can't. I'm swamped," I lied. "Listen, Leona is sending a call through. I gotta go." I ended the call before Dustin said bye and tried to press further into getting me to go with him. I'd gone a few times in the past—just as friends with Silvie—

but crap, that was not what I wanted to do at this juncture. I blew out a breath. It was easier to avoid my friends while Quinn and I carried on with this affair. The guilt didn't seem to claw at me so much. I pressed the button for Leona. "I can't take a call right now. Take a message for me. Thank you."

Taking a piece of advice from Q, I sent a few emails to a couple of my clients, hoping to get home in the next thirty minutes. It would be great to go out to dinner. Was there anywhere within a fifty-mile radius that I wouldn't run into someone I knew?

I sent Quinn a text: *Are you free tonight?*

Quinn: *Maybe. Why?*

Me: *Let's go out to dinner.*

Quinn: *Where?*

Me: *How about at The Red River?*

Quinn: *Or we could cook at your place...*

Me: *Next time. Tonight I want to take you out.*

I felt comfortable with that. It was up in the mountains, far enough away on a Tuesday night that the chances of running into anyone were slim to none. By the time we got up there, it would be past traditional dinner time.

Quinn: *Is this our first official date?*

Me: *Technically, I suppose. But I consider your birthday our first official date.*

Quinn: *You do????*

She sent me an emoji of a birthday cake, the yellow face that had little red hearts instead of eyes, a peach, and an eggplant. Her emojis were confusing. I could pretend to guess what they meant, but seriously, I had zero ideas. What did fruit and veggies have to do with birthdays? I was pretty sure she wasn't the type to make those shredded zucchini cakes.

Me: *You don't?*

Now I felt like a fuckhead for thinking we'd had a date. We'd slept together. That had to count for some kind of date, didn't it?

Quinn: *I never sleep with someone on the first date.*

Me: *I'm not just any someone. I'm someone special.*

Quinn: *Damn right you are. Do you want me to meet you at Red River or will we be driving up together?*

Me: *Driving up together, I hope.*

Quinn: *I'll be at your house in twenty-five minutes. That will give you a chance to get home. Cause I know you're still at the office.*

One thing about Quinn was that she was a smart, observant cookie.

Me: *Sounds good.*

Quinn: *See you soon.*

Me: *Oh, and Q?*

Quinn: *Yeah?*

Me: *Make sure you wear one of those dresses tonight.*

Quinn: *Yes, sir.*

Me: *And no panties.*

I added the emoji with the hearts for eyes.

She sent back one single emoji. A blue splash of water. Wet. I could totally understand that emoji. The other ones, I would have to ask about.

By the time I got home, I barely had time to freshen up before Quinn arrived. I didn't even second guess that she hadn't followed my request to not wear panties. She wasn't wearing any. She was bold like that.

I opened my garage door, and she pulled her Jeep inside. When she stepped out, I caught a glimpse of her upper thighs. Her dress was tight this time. Black and short. Not something she would wear at the office.

I pulled her into my arms, but my kiss was light and brief. She'd wound me up so fucking tight today that I knew if I allowed it, we would never make it out of here. "Come on, babe."

We got into my Lexus and took off. Quinn took the liberty of changing the channel on my radio before giving up altogether and hooking up her phone to my Bluetooth. "You don't mind, do you?"

I laughed. "Too late to ask my opinion now."

She shrugged. "I knew you wouldn't care. Here. This is my latest playlist I made on Spotify. Ever since you and I started..."

She drifted off, but I took the liberty of answering for her. "Dating?"

"Is that what we're doing?"

"Would you rather we just fuck when we feel like it?" I glanced over at her. I would do what she wanted, but there was something to be said for having Quinn all to myself.

She was staring out the window, rubbing the pads of her thumbs.

"Talk to me. What do you want?"

Her eyes were big, piercing. "I'm not sure what I want. I know I want you. I know you're the man to fulfill all of my sexual desires." She glanced out the window and back. "But I know you, and I can't be much more than that either. At least never in real life."

I squeezed the steering wheel tightly. She was right. As it stood now, we were destined to just this fling. I kept my eyes on the road and turned into the massive parking lot of Red River. There were four cars in the lot and a few in the back where the staff usually parked.

Fling? I unclenched my jaw. No reason to have this ruin our first evening out. We had enough in this secret life of ours for now. I wasn't going to waste it. I shut off my engine and ran a hand up her thigh. "You wearing panties, Q?"

She smirked and playfully pushed my hand away. "I guess you'll have to find out inside, won't you?"

I chuckled. "Look. Sorry to have used the word *dating*. All I know is that I do want to keep doing this with you for a while. We've barely begun in my eyes."

"Me too. Dating makes it sound like there will be more, and I have to remind myself that you and I can't have more than this."

I shifted in my seat. I couldn't say anything to that. Did I like it? No, I really didn't. But she hit the nail on the head. There couldn't be more. I hadn't seen Greg very mad over all the years I'd known him, but I could envision the look on his face if he ever found out I was screwing his youngest daughter. "Let's eat."

We made our way inside, where we were seated at a booth that was semi-enclosed should anyone I know be lurking around.

"You first." I gestured for Quinn to slide into the booth. Once she did, I slid in next to her. She tried to slide away to give me more room. I gripped her thigh. "You're not going anywhere. I plan to fully figure out whether you have panties under that dress."

A throat cleared. "What can I get you two for drinks?" Our waiter loomed over us, waiting for our answers.

I glanced at Quinn, whose cheeks were of the brightest shade of red. She was ignoring the waiter entirely, her nose stuck in the menu. I laughed. "Water is great for us for now."

"Certainly." He walked away.

Quinn put down her menu and looked me in the eye. "How embarrassing."

"He's probably heard worse. If he even heard us at all." My hand slid up her thigh. "The only thing with you and I is that even though I was married, there are a lot of things I haven't experienced. Most of the kinkier things you want to do, but this—" I edged my fingers up her dress, getting closer to figuring out her panty situation. "Holly would have never allowed me to do stuff like this to her."

The look on Quinn's face was classic. "Why? What's the big deal?"

That was exactly the question I was asking myself, twenty years too late. "Not sure. That just wasn't Holly."

"She did seem a little too uptight, looking back on it."

I gave a dry laugh.

Our waiter came back with our waters. "I'll come back in a few minutes to take your orders. Any questions so far?"

"Could I see the dessert menu?" Quinn asked.

The waiter and I were slightly taken aback, but he recovered quickly. "Sure thing." He disappeared briefly before setting the menu in front of Quinn. "Here you are."

"Dessert first?" This woman intrigued the fuck out of me.

"No, just dessert."

"You're not going to have a steak or a salad?"

She shrugged. "No. I'm fine. This will be good."

I settled back in my seat. My first instinct was to insist that dinner was first. That she should have food then dessert. But the more I thought about it, the more I realized Quinn was right. Why not order whatever the hell she wanted? She looked it over, her mouth curved into a smile, and she set the dessert menu down. Her eyes met mine. "Give me that."

I opened the dessert menu, perused it, and found something I would enjoy. "What are you ordering?"

"Bananas Foster. What about you?"

My mouth watered, already knowing how good it would taste. "Same."

"Good."

"Very good." I put the menus in a pile. I could feel Quinn's eyes on me. "Why are you staring at me?"

"Because you're sexy. And I can't believe we're doing this. And I'm sorry about Holly. That she was so uptight about sex and stuff."

"I never understood it." That was the fucking truth. It was always me initiating sex with Holly. Always me who wanted more. Always me who tried to play more, to be bolder about things. Perhaps that was why Holly had decided I wasn't the man for her. Too much sex on the brain. But I couldn't believe I was the only man around who thought about sex and wanted to explore as much as I did.

"I haven't had a lot of great sex. But I'm more than willing to try. To experiment. To do stuff. I don't get how people don't like sex. They must not be horny. Or have the right person to spark the interest." Quinn's shoulder drooped like there'd been a death in the family.

Our waiter came back. "Ready to order?"

"We'll both have the bananas Foster. Nothing else."

"Excellent choice. We will bring it out."

"That was easy," I said.

"And fun. Admit it." Quinn pressed her thigh into mine.

"It was fun. It did feel freeing to not have to order something because that's the norm. I'll probably pay for it later when I'm starved for real food."

"Yeah, bananas are real food. Plus, you could tell the waiter you want an order to go. No biggie."

I was already nodding in agreement. Wow. Who was I?

I was having dessert for dinner and leaning toward putting a fifty-dollar steak in a to-go container. Even in my perpetual bachelordom, I'd always either grilled myself or gotten fast food to-go. The idea of ordering a fifty-dollar meal and eating it in the privacy or convenience of my own home had never occurred to me.

"What is this?" Quinn squealed, squeezing my thigh.

Our waiter rolled a cart up next to our booth, equipped with a grill and all the ingredients for our dessert. I glanced at Quinn. "Have you never had this before?"

She shook her head. "Not like this. One time, but it was premade, and they served it to us in bowls. But this, what is this?" She giggled and squirmed in her seat.

"The joys of ordering bananas Foster." Our waiter added butter and brown sugar before stirring them together with long, slow strokes.

It was hard to watch him when my eyes kept watching Quinn and her absolute excitement. She was beaming, hands clasped together. Every time she leaned forward, her dress hitched up a little, giving me ideas about what I wanted to do to her while she was enjoying her dessert.

"Now for the big part." The water tossed in all of the sliced bananas and poured alcohol into the pan. He lit it with his lighter, and a gust of heat warmed my face.

"Oh my gosh!" Quinn's grip on my thigh went from relaxed to squeezing me every other second. "I never knew this was how to really do it. I had no idea."

I settled back in my seat, enjoying the beauty of this moment. A warm liquid settled inside all the cracks of my heart. Quinn's innocent outlook and the way she got excited so easily were enough to have me questioning why I hadn't been lucky enough to meet someone with her same zest for life when I was younger. My heart pinched a little at how

I'd been so enamored with Holly, but the truth was, it hadn't been Holly. It had been my future. And Holly had happened to be a part of that.

That was probably why she'd divorced me. She'd figured it out a lot sooner than I had.

"Here you are." The waiter set down our bowls of already-melting vanilla ice cream with the wholesome banana topping.

The realization that I hadn't been the best husband because I hadn't been in love with Holly settled heavily in my stomach. Next to me, Quinn dug into her dessert, moaning and groaning like she did when I went down on her. "It sounds like you like this more than you like when I go down on you."

Her spoon stopped midway to her mouth. "Huh?"

"Your moans and groans. I'm surprised our waiter isn't over here thinking we're having sex."

Her cheeks flushed pink. "Is that how I sound when you're down there? How embarrassing. I'll try not to be so dramatic next time."

"I like dramatic." I slipped my finger under her dress. *Bingo.* "I like no panties too."

Q's eyes darted around the restaurant. "You can't do this here." She nodded to my untouched dessert. "Eat."

I shook my head. I didn't want my dessert. I wanted Quinn for dessert. I flicked her clit with my fingers. Her legs spread a teensy bit apart. "That's it. You eat. While I play."

"I don't think..." Her voice trailed off when I pressed a finger inside her. Quinn never disappointed in the wet department. "Oh, goodness. I should..."

I pulled my hand from between her legs and licked her off my fingers. I raised an eyebrow at the look she was giving me. "You taste better than that." I nodded to my untouched dessert.

"I don't think so. This tastes like heaven. Perfection in a bowl. It glides over my tongue so easily."

"You do all those things for me."

Her cheeks blazed red. Maybe she wasn't ready to hear all that, but I didn't care.

"Don't act shy. You know you taste better to me than any dessert."

Quinn scarfed down her bowl, and when she finished, I pushed my bowl toward her. "Eat." That was all the command I gave.

"I'm the manager here at Red River. I trust your food was well?" A tall, thin man stood at our table, his eyes shifting from Quinn to me.

"Indeed. Thank you."

"Are we celebrating anything special?" He pointed to my almost-empty bowl sitting in front of a shocked Quinn. "Dad spoiling you tonight?"

Her cheeks went bright red again. She looked to me as if I should correct the manager, but when I didn't say anything, she got that rebellious look on her face.

Oh God.

"Daddy is always good to me."

The manager's face went bright red, and he shuffled away. I busted up with laughter. "Come on, little girl. Let's go. You keep that Daddy shit up, and I won't be buying you bananas Foster anymore."

We paid, and I guided her to the parking lot.

"That was embarrassing," Quinn said. "Not only had he almost busted us with your fingers between my thighs, but *dad?*"

I wasn't sure how I felt about that, to be honest. Twenty

years difference. There were obviously a lot of physical differences between the two of us as far as our age gap. Hell, I could bet she still got carded for alcohol, whereas it was evident I was an older man. We slid into the Lexus, and I turned to her. "Does that bother you?"

"What? That he thought you were my dad?"

"We have a lot of years between us, Q. Some could argue I'm halfway through living while you're just getting started." *Shit.* Was this bothering me? It was easy to forget about our age difference when we were alone. Thinking about how I would feel if I learned Greg was sleeping with Cera, made me feel guilty as fuck.

"Honestly?" Her eyes were on fire, bright and unwavering. She started shaking her head. "That's one of the many things I like about you. That you are older. Confident. Experienced. Wise. I like how I know what I'm getting with you."

I pulled out onto the highway and pointed the car toward home. "What do you mean?"

"I like how there isn't any drama with you. That you aren't judgmental about my sexual desires. That you aren't sitting at home playing video games and carrying on like they're life. I like how every night isn't a party night for you. I like how you have money." She blushed. "Not that I'm a gold digger. I appreciate that you aren't scrambling around for fifty dollars to try to fill up your gas tank. That you aren't living with your parents." Quinn touched my forearm, sending tingles across my skin. "I especially like how long you can go before…"

I raised an eyebrow at her. "Before what?"

"Before you come. You're the first guy I've ever been with to care so much about my pleasure. It's flattering."

"You deserve the best." I chuckled. "And honestly, I

couldn't imagine it being any other way. What kind of jackass gets off before their woman? No manly man. That's for fucks' sure."

Her hand traveled to my thigh and across my dick. She squeezed.

"You, young lady, are in for quite the sexual experience."

She gave me a cocky grin. "Am I? Or are you too?"

11

QUINN

"Unbutton them."

He glanced at me before snaking around a curve. "You want me to unzip my pants while I'm driving?"

I smiled at his surprise. Like no one in this world had ever been given head or been jacked off while in the driver's seat. I nodded.

He unbuckled his pants but left his dick in his underwear. I squeezed it again. "I love touching it. Holding it. It's so big." It was truly more than I'd ever had the pleasure of dealing with. He was so much more in every aspect, and I loved that. He was the ultimate package. "Always so ready for me." Funny thing was that I didn't feel a lick of guilt about being with him.

"It's easy to be always ready for someone who has the same desires and stamina as I do," Jason teased.

I nodded. "Truth."

I pulled his dick out of his briefs while he kept us on the road. I knew he wanted to look at me. Every chance he got, I could feel his eyes on me. I stroked him, gripping his heavy shaft, first hard then soft, from base to tip. His legs tightened beneath my wrist.

"Could you come like this?" I stroked him in slow, hard movements up and down.

"No."

I unbuckled my seat belt and got onto my knees, reaching over the gear shift. "But I bet you could come like this." I lowered my mouth over his burgeoning erection.

"Ahh." His hand topped my head, resting gently against my hair. His hips arched up, driving his cock into my mouth.

I took him deeply. I sucked him harder when he flexed his hips into my mouth. I took him in as far as I could, then he growled. I wanted to be the best for him. I wanted to give him everything he'd been giving me.

"Quinn." His hand fisted my hair, and he shocked the hell out of me when he raised his hips and fucked my mouth—thrust after thrust after thrust before he collapsed with his release. His groan echoed between us. How was I ever going to get enough of him?

I CARRIED that question with me well into the night and the next morning while I sat with my dad at breakfast.

"You're losing weight, Quinn. Gotta eat more." He set a steaming plate of hash browns and bacon in front of me.

I frowned. There was no way. I glanced down at my clothes—standard Quinn summer attire. Tank top and jean shorts. I recalled pulling my shorts on this morning and the small gap between my stomach when I buttoned them. "I'm not trying to." Was it the extracurricular activities? "I had two desserts yesterday." I reached for the bacon and dumped more hash browns than I would normally eat onto my plate. "Maybe it's work."

"How's working with Jason? Haven't heard you talk about him as much lately." My dad was busting eggs into a pan, his back to me. "For a while there, you were gung-ho, talking about him every day."

That was true. That was before he'd had his tongue between my legs. What if I laid it out for my dad right now? *I'm fucking Jason. He's by far the best guy I've ever been with, and I want to keep exploring wherever this takes us.*

"Q?"

I blinked.

My dad was still standing at the stove, but he was turned back to face me. "Something wrong at the office? You've already been there a few weeks."

Why is this happening to me now? I loved my dad. I'd never had any secrets to keep from him, and all of a sudden, this one secret was ready to bubble out of my throat. Convenient. Especially when last night, I hadn't felt any sort of guilt. I swallowed. If I told my dad now, it would blindside Jason. I couldn't do that to him.

"No. Everything is fine, actually." My stomach tilted at my big secret. His good daughter was all sorts of not good right now. Could a father ever accept that his daughter was fucking one of his very best friends? Surely, it happened. I couldn't be the first in this world to be having an illicit love affair with a man twenty years older than me.

My dad flipped two eggs onto my plate, eyeing me. "Talk to me, Q. I know something is up with you. Let's get it out in the open." He flipped his eggs onto his plate and sat in front of me. "You're not already regretting working for Jason, are you? He's a good guy, but I really don't know what he's like at work. How he treats his employees."

"He spanks them." My mouth dropped. *Did I really just say that?*

My dad's head fell back into a fit of laughter.

Oh shit. I smiled. Then started laughing with my dad. "Jason is fine to work with. I don't want to mess anything up. I want to be perfect for him." I cut up my eggs with my fork. That was all true enough. It was simply not in the context my dad was thinking. "I want to make him happy. I'm worried about not passing my bar exam." I shoveled bits of egg into my mouth. "I'm a little stressed. I want it all to work well between us."

"Shit. It will. Don't stress. He's a great guy. Always takes care of one of his own. You know you're like a daughter to him."

Weird tingles spread across my skin. I wanted to be one of Jason's own, but I knew he didn't think of me as a daughter. I held in a laugh at the thought of calling Jason Daddy. Maybe this was a new kink we should try? I shoveled in some hash browns and followed it up with a drink of my orange juice. "I'm surprised he's never remarried or anything." *Great, now I'm fishing.*

"I think Holly messed him up. How do you stay married for twenty-some years and then divorce in an instant? Jason is perfect at being alone. He might crave companionship, but I'm sure you've noticed how many hours he pulls in at the office. He's working all the time. Even when we go up to his cabin, he works. Having a wife or significant other this late in the game would be foolish for him."

"Is that what he thinks?" I asked.

My dad shrugged. "How could he not? That was a small part of Holly's complaint when she left. He's a workaholic."

I left it at that. Jason wasn't being a workaholic with me

around. In fact, it was kind of almost the opposite. He rarely worked late, especially on the nights we were together. When we were in the office, I forced Jason to take a lunch break with me under the guise that it was a working lunch where we talked about stuff he wanted me to research or return calls. It was our daily planning session unless he had court.

I helped my dad with the dishes and thanked him for breakfast. That night was their monthly business soiree, where it was entirely rare for anyone to talk about real business. I didn't get why they didn't just call it a party.

I sent a text to Jason: *You coming over tonight?*

Me: *I told my dad you spank your employees.*

Me: *Truth!!*

I included a little purple devil emoji, and instantaneously, my phone buzzed in my hands. *Jason.* "Yes, Counselor?"

"Tell me you did not tell Greg I spank my employees." His voice was low and quiet. Not angry, but I definitely had his attention.

My thighs quivered with desperation for him. God, I was such a horny mess when it came to this man. I took the stairs to my room, running down them as fast as I could, and flopped onto my bed. "I did. Does that deserve another spanking?" I started rubbing my clit in small circles.

"Depends on what he said."

"He laughed. Thought I was teasing." I continued to rub. "But I know the truth. You like spanking me, don't you, Jason?" I went for the sexiest voice I could muster. "Where are you right now?"

A long silence followed my question. "Eating brunch with Cera and Christina."

I could hear shuffling like maybe he was moving to a

more private spot. "Answer the question. Do you like spanking me?"

A growl escaped his mouth. "Fuck yeah."

"Do you have any idea how many times I've thought about you spanking my bare ass? About how many times I've gotten myself off with my vibrator, pretending you tied me up to your bed."

"Don't stop touching yourself." *His voice.*

"How did you know?" I trailed my fingertips up my stomach and to my braless nipples, all the while smiling because he knew.

"I can hear the change in your voice. You've done it since the very first time I got you off."

I wanted to ask where exactly he was having brunch with his daughters, but I didn't want to break this spell. It was so intoxicating. "Will you tie me up tonight?"

"I'll be at your house. Business party."

"So?" I pressed my fingers back to my clit. "I'm imagining my fingers are yours right now. I want to come all over your fingers so bad."

"Do it," he demanded. "Hurry up."

I pressed my fingers inside of me and started grinding against my palm. "We have so many things to do and so little time."

"Who said we had to stop anytime soon?"

Ah fuck. His voice. It was enough to send me over the edge. "I hope we don't. I don't want to."

"You still touching yourself, Q? You're getting kind of chatty." I could hear other stuff in the background, then he said, "Keep going."

I was so close. "Tell me something dirty. Anything. Say anything," I pleaded. I ground against my palm harder, wishing it were him.

"I want you in a skirt tonight. No panties. No bra. Your pussy and ass are mine tonight. You are mine. I'm going to ravage that pussy any chance I get tonight. You hear me?"

Fuck yes. Loud and clear. My pussy clenched. My toes curled. I was on the brink.

"Tell me you're coming all over those pretty fingers of yours."

The dam inside me exploded. A whimper escaped my throat. "I'm. Coming. Right. Now."

"Good girl. Don't forget what I said about tonight."

Then he was gone, and I was staring at my ceiling, wondering how in the hell I'd gotten so lucky to experience all of these firsts with someone as amazing as Jason. I was safe with him. My desires were safe with him.

I was pretty sure he was bluffing about tonight because there was no way we could do anything with so many people here, but I went in search of my best outfit that I could wear without panties or a bra.

"I DON'T GET my results until October. It's the longest wait ever." My eyes did another once-over the house, making sure Jason hadn't snuck in yet.

"Are you happy you changed jobs now? Jason has been pretty focused lately." Dustin drained his beer and set his glass on the counter.

"Yeah, I'm happy. Why wouldn't I be? Jason's a good guy."

Dustin shrugged. "He is. But he can be a hothead at times."

"Jason? I'm around him a lot. I wouldn't call him a hothead."

Dustin chuckled. "With you, he's probably not too bad."

"Are you telling Quinn to get a new job?" Jason's smooth voice behind me sent shivers across my skin.

I resisted the urge to turn around and hug him. "He was."

Dustin raised his eyebrows at me. "Thanks, Quinn. I see where your loyalties stand."

Jason moved up to the counter, and I caught my first glimpse of him. He was in a white buttoned shirt with a purple tie the exact color of the blindfold he'd given me. Did he recognize the similarity when he picked it out today? I hadn't seen him at the office all day, and I hoped the color hadn't been lost on him. Butterflies soared in my stomach. I met his gaze, and everyone else in the room seemed to disappear.

Jason took his tie in his hand, giving the tip a few strokes before his mouth tilted up and his dimples came out. "I'm her boss. She knows where her loyalties lie."

Had I even really lived before Jason and I started this forbidden love affair? "He said you have a temper—which I haven't ever witnessed over twenty-five years."

Jason barked out a laugh. "You really trying to feed her that shit? At least give her something that slightly resembles me."

Dustin waved a hand in between us. "She knows I'm messing with her. You need someone like Quinn at the office."

I was pulled away by other guests, and it was a few hours later when I caught Jason looking at me from across the room. His eyes flitted from my legs, perusing slowly up to my thighs and breasts before they landed on my face. He smiled.

I tilted my head toward the basement then quietly took

the hallway and went downstairs, hoping he would follow. I shut off the main light but left the single one on above the wet bar. The jukebox was plugged in, blazing neon colors, but nothing poured from the speakers. If Jason came down, I would be able to hear his arrival on the two creaky steps.

It felt like forever. My anticipation went from a hundred percent to sixty. Five minutes ticked by. I straightened up the bar, throwing a crumpled napkin away and washing a cup that was left in the sink. Twelve minutes. I considered pouring myself a drink. Eighteen minutes later, I'd given up and was no longer wet from the idea of what we could accomplish down here in a short period of time. Not to mention the risk of getting caught. If I was totally honest, it was that risk that made me want this so desperately. It was probably too obvious for him to come to the basement, especially if he was in the middle of a conversation with my dad.

The steps creaked, spreading joy through my bones. *Finally.* I leaned against the countertop, flooded with desire, waiting for him to round the corner. He was already undoing his tie. His gaze met mine, and he put a single finger to his lips.

Oh, we're going to do this in the quiet.

He'd already rolled up his sleeves. His hair was a bit disheveled like he'd been running a hand through it.

"Glad you could make it."

"Me fucking too." His eyes scanned the room like he was looking for something, then his gaze settled on the workout cage across the room. "Follow me."

"Should we... uh... go in my room?"

Jason shook his head. He proceeded to move the workout bench so that it was in the center of one of the metal brackets that made up part of the cage. "You're not wearing panties, are you?"

Instead of waiting for a response, he pulled me toward him and pressed his mouth into mine. Rough. Fast. It was exactly what I wanted. "We're safe down here."

"No one comes down much anymore."

He stepped back, his tie now dangling from his hand. "You okay if I tie you up?"

I couldn't think of anything better right now. "You're not afraid we might get caught?" Muffled laughter floated down the steps. Glasses clanked. But since I'd shut off the lights in the stairwell, we were likely safe—as long as we hurried.

He chuckled. "Trust me, this is going to be quick."

Thrills shot through my bloodstream. I loved how much I wound him up. I loved that he was on the same page as me. Being tied up to this machine while he fucked me, knowing there was a chance we could get caught? I wasn't going to last long either.

"Hands up, Q."

I swallowed and climbed onto the bench. My skirt bunched around my ass, and Jason's intake of breath had me spreading my legs apart while I leaned against the metal bar.

"Like this?" I was standing on top of the bench, leaning against the bar, my hands above my head.

He nodded then tied my wrists to the bar. "Tell me if it hurts. Tell me if I start hurting you in any way, okay?"

I nodded.

"Say it out loud, Quinn." He tightened the slack on the tie, binding my wrists to the machine.

"I will tell you if you hurt me."

"And I'll stop." His cock strained against the fabric of his trousers.

I tugged the restraint. *Definitely not going anywhere.* I glanced at the stairs. "I'm dying, Jason."

Instead of standing on the weight bench... in my haze of lust, I hadn't thought through what he was actually going to do to me. He straddled the bench and scooted toward me. I was wound tight with anticipation. Arousal. Even a little bit of fear at someone coming down those steps.

"Stop moving your legs," he growled.

"Put your fucking mouth on my pussy, and I will," I growled back.

He smiled at me, and at least if I died from pent-up desire right this second, I would die with the impression of his sexy dimples planted firmly in my mind.

He lifted my legs over his shoulders. "I got you, Q."

He did.

He always had me.

He devoured me. His tongue swiped up and down. His teeth tugged my clit. His mouth did magical things to me that I swore I was never going to get enough of. He knew my body. He knew what I needed, and when he speared me with his fingers, I came all over his mouth. My wrists ached. I let out a moan. My legs quivered atop his shoulders, but he was careful not to let me go.

"What about you?" A whisper barely escaped my throat.

"I'm next." He teased. He squeezed my thighs. "You okay?"

Quivers still vibrated through my body, but yeah, I was good. I nodded.

The unmistakable sound of the floorboards creaking had me flying off Jason's shoulders, tugging my bound wrists. "Someone is coming," I whisper yelled, tugging again, but it was fucking useless. My skirt was bunched up still, and Jason stood on the bench, trying to untie me. "Put my skirt down."

It was as if he didn't know what he should do first. He hesitated, and adrenaline shot through me. Yeah, the tie. He was right. He continued to fumble with my restraint. Was it my dad? A fucking coworker of Jason's? Hannah? Finally, the tie gave around my wrists, but I was still tangled up. Like he'd given up and accepted the fact that we were caught in the act, Jason turned and shielded my lower half.

The lights switched on. We turned to the stairs.

"Am I seeing what I fucking think I'm seeing?"

12

JASON

Dustin's smirk was enough to piss me off, but logically, I only had myself to blame. I'd known meeting Quinn down here was risky as fuck. "It's not what you think."

Quinn gave a big tug behind me, and I knew she'd finally freed herself from the tie. My priority was to untie her, but obviously, I should have pulled her skirt down. She moved behind me, shimmying her skirt down.

"It looks like it's exactly what I'm thinking. What the fuck is wrong with you, man? You're fucking *little Quinn?*" His face was mottled with rage. My stomach plummeted.

"I'm not a child," Quinn said from behind me.

"We didn't plan for this to happen," I said.

"Does your father know?" He pushed a hand through his hair. "By the looks on your faces, he has no clue. No, Dustin, of course he doesn't know. She's twenty years younger than he is." He pointed an angry finger at me.

I stepped off the bench and held my hand out to help her down. Her fingers trembled in mine. I couldn't even offer up an apology because I wasn't sorry about us. But what had I been thinking? This was so stupid. Disgust flooded my veins as I realized that I had jeopardized every-thing—Quinn's relationship with her dad and our friend-ship—for the thrill of getting caught.

"No. My dad doesn't know." Quinn's voice was shaky. "You can't tell him."

I didn't even know where to start. For once I was entirely unsure of how to diffuse the situation. It was best to keep my mouth shut.

Dustin stepped toward us, meeting us in the middle. He better not make some smart, shitty comment about this, or I would fucking punch him. One comment about Quinn and her sexuality, I would lay him on the floor in two seconds.

"How long has this been going on?" His voice was more curious than anything else.

"A month or so." I glanced at Quinn.

"Yeah, that's about right." Her voice was less shaky. I held up her wrists, making sure I hadn't hurt her with my tie. "I'm okay. Just a few red marks. But I'm good," she assured me.

This was reckless. Dumb. I should have known better. Had that been Greg...

Dustin was shaking his head. "This might be the dumbest thing you've ever done. We've all had a good run. Probably going to end when Greg learns the truth. He's going to kill you when he finds out."

"He doesn't have to find out." Quinn's voice was low.

"I can't keep something like this from him. He'd kill me."

"Just mind your own business for now. Give us time. We'll tell him," I said, all the while staring at Quinn.

Her lips quirked up into her little rebellious grin, and I

braced myself for whatever was going to come out of her mouth.

"You can't say anything. Please don't. I know you may not approve, and that's fine to have your own opinion. But I'm an adult, and so is he. You wouldn't tell my dad about any other relationship I had, so please don't tell him about this one. Jason and I will tell him. Just give us that. Our own time. Please."

I stayed silent. I didn't want to sway Dustin one way or the other. If he felt his moral obligation was that important, I sure wasn't going to try to convince him otherwise.

For a minute, the three of us stood there in silence.

"Fine. I won't say anything." He folded his arms over his chest. "But you're wrong about one thing. I would tell him if I thought you were in a wrong relationship." He put his hands to his sides. "But since I don't think there is anything nefarious about this except a good time, I won't say anything. Under one condition. When this goes public, leave my fucking name out of it. I never knew this happened."

"Not going to say a word." Quinn rushed to Dustin and threw her arms around his neck. "I knew I could count on you."

He didn't hug her back at first, eyeing me like I was going to attack him.

When I shrugged, he slowly raised his arms around her lower back.

Quinn smiled. "I'll be in my room."

When she shut her door, Dustin attacked. "What are you thinking? You know she's young. Impressionable. This isn't going to end well for her when you're done with her."

I put my hands up. "Stop. I'm not planning on hurting her."

"You planning on not hurting her and hurting her because that's just how things work aren't the same. Nothing will be the same after this."

"It won't." That was no lie. My heart was the fullest it had ever been in my entire life. I was changed. For good. For the better. No matter what happened, I would hold this near and dear to my heart. Forever. "She's pretty amazing."

"You have *feelings* for her?" Dustin raised an eyebrow and smirked. He paced the floor, running his hand through his hair. He looked at me sideways. "This can't end well. I don't see how it could."

I made no response. My shoulders went up. I didn't know what to say.

"Think about it. I'll be upstairs." Dustin walked away, leaving me to ponder the situation. All I knew was that I wanted to be with her badly.

"Q?" I leaned my forehead against her door.

"Yeah?"

My throat got thick with emotion. "I, ah... thank you for making my lonely life better." I swallowed at her silence. "I know that sounds crazy—"

My head fell when she swung the door open. She'd changed into some tiny little pajama bottoms and a matching tank top with flying pigs all over it. She ran into my arms and tugged my head down. Her mouth met mine. Her kiss was slow and sweet. Her tongue cascaded along my teeth and across my tongue. Gentle. Unhurried.

Perhaps she was just as grateful for our relationship. Even if it was unconventional. Crazy, even.

She pulled away. "I should be thanking you for bringing me out of my shell."

This made me laugh. "Q, you have never been in a

shell. You've always marched to the beat of your own drum. You just needed the right line to figure it out."

I turned away and went upstairs, afraid that if I didn't leave, we would get caught in the act a second time, and it would be by her father.

13

QUINN

"You can make me new files for each of these cases. Some of them are past clients, but I like to organize by date. Like for this one, put her last name Bland and then the date on this paper on there."

I took the stack from Jason. "This won't take me very long. But don't you have anything else that's... I don't know, more important for me to do than just naming folders?"

Jason gave me a hard look—his "thinking look," I liked to call it. "The best part about being my legal clerk is that every job you do is valuable to me. It could be simple things like getting me a chai latte or naming folders or something much more extreme. But all of it is important. So, for now, this is all I need." He gave me his smile that was full of lewd thoughts. "Thank you."

I stalked back to my office. Jason had court every day this past week, and I was knee-deep in my own work. We'd hardly seen one another since getting caught by Dustin. Finally, it was Friday afternoon, and Jason and I had the office all to ourselves even though he was still busy.

I shut my office door and leaned against it. I was dying for some alone time with Jason.

Me: *We good?*

I added the smiley emoji with heart eyes. It took a few minutes for him to respond.

Jason: *More than good. You know that.*

Me: *It's just... we haven't had a chance to talk much since...*

Jason: *Since we got caught?*

He added two laughing emojis that were crying.

Me: *Ha ha. Yes.*

Me: *Now... what are you doing tonight?*

Jason: *You?*

Me: *I would love that.*

Jason: *I want you to come over. I want you to use your blindfold.*

Me: *I thought you were going to beg to fuck my ass.*

Jason: *I don't have to beg for that. You and I both know it's gonna be mine.*

He was absolutely right. My virgin ass was going to be his. In time. Some day.

Me: *What time?*

Jason: *Eight? I have some errands to run and then I'll be there. In fact, the code is 8774 to the garage. Feel free to pull in. I might be a little late.*

Quinn: *Ok!*

When I got to his house at 7:53, I sent him a text.

Me: *I pulled in the garage. I'm waiting.*

I followed up with a picture of me wearing the new lingerie I'd bought for us. It was purple lace that framed my breasts and pussy like chains of ribbon, leaving me completely exposed. He only got to preview the upper half.

Jason: *Where did you get that?*

Me: *It so happens that it matches my blindfold perfectly.*

Jason: *I love it. I can't wait to tear it off you.*

Jason: *I thought it was our blindfold.*

I decided to surprise him and went inside. The blindfold was where we'd left it in his nightstand. I got undressed so I was only in my lingerie and made quick work of tying the blindfold around my head. I crawled onto his bed and waited.

I must have fallen asleep because when I woke up, Jason was trailing his fingers across my skin in slow sweeping gestures. "I could come home to this every day."

I leaned up onto my elbows. "I fell asleep. What time is it?"

"Almost nine. Sorry I'm late. I got caught up on working on a case. I texted you to let you know."

"It's okay." I stretched. "What do you think?"

"That I'm in love." I could hear the smile in his voice.

The ever-present butterflies swirled in my belly at his words. *Love.* I know he didn't mean it *that* way, but my body had other plans, yearning to hear these kinds of words from him forever.

His fingers glided slowly over the mound of one of my tits to the center of my chest then up and over to the next one, leaving a trail of tickles. "You are magnificent."

"I missed you this week." I reached for his hand and kissed his palm.

"Me too. Sorry we haven't gotten to spend much time together." He moved his hand down my stomach. "Does this thing open at the bottom?"

I spread my legs apart for him to see. I heard his intake of breath. "You like that?"

"Don't move." The pressure of where he was sitting shifted, indicating he was standing.

"Tell me what you're doing."

"I took my shoes off. And now I'm going to take off my tie and the rest of my clothes."

"Leave them on."

"Everything?" he asked.

"For now." I touched myself between my legs, knowing he was watching. "It turns me on when you're in your work clothes."

His chuckle was low and sensual. "You can't even see me."

"I know. But I can feel your clothes brush against my skin. Imagine how you'll look between my legs."

Again, he chuckled. "Is that where you want me?"

"Please. Just the thought..." I kept circling my clit. This man made me so brazen. So hot.

"I rather like what I'm looking at right now." He pressed into the bed. His cologne teased my senses. His warm breath tickled my ear. "Imagine what I'm seeing right now." He nipped my earlobe. "Stick your fingers inside, Q. I want to watch you make yourself come."

I turned toward him, seeking his mouth, trying to imagine what he was seeing. Me. With my beautiful purple blindfold and matching ribbons tied around my body. Lying in the center of his bed. Touching myself. Even I couldn't disagree that the image sounded beautiful. Made me feel sexy. Powerful. In charge.

"I feel beautiful," I admitted.

He sucked in my bottom lip and let it go on a slurp. "You should. You're a goddess. How did I get so lucky to end up with you?"

His words sent flutters over my heart. I know he didn't mean permanently, but a part of me wanted permanent. A part of me wanted to experience this high-on-life feeling forever. A part of me wanted to ask him if he did too. I wanted to live this way with him. In our own little world. Safe with one another. Comfortable that he would cherish me. Give me all the things I fantasized about without shame or guilt. "We both got lucky."

"Don't stop. Keep touching yourself." He brushed his mouth against mine. "Tell me something, Q."

I tried to focus on the task at hand—working on my clit, teasing it, caressing it. "What's that?"

"What do you truly desire? What do you want from this relationship?"

"You already know. Everything you're giving me."

"Has anything changed for you since we started this?" His hands were roaming over my breasts, teasing my nipples.

It was hard to talk and think about his question. I couldn't concentrate on both tasks. I was so close. He pulled away, and the bed rose from the loss of his body. His belt buckle clanked in the silence. The teeth of his zipper broke apart slowly. The bed dipped again but on both sides of me.

My lips parted.

"Good girl." He brushed his cock along my lips. His skin was warm and soft. I licked his crown like he was a Popsicle. "Keep touching yourself." He teased me with his cock, not putting it in my mouth, and when I tried, he would pull back. "You're not focusing, Q. It's never taken you this long."

My frustration mounted. I was focusing, damn it. I couldn't get my tongue to stop lashing out for a taste of him. I teased my clit and inserted a finger inside, wishing it were his fingers. I was totally focusing. Finally, his cock touched my lips, and I licked.

"You want this cock?"

I nodded. God, yes. That was all I wanted. All the time. "Please."

I opened my mouth and was rewarded with his fat, delicious cock against the flat of my tongue.

My thighs began to quiver. I rubbed harder. My clit pulsated against fingers. My mouth was full of Jason as he fucked me. I exploded. My orgasm was so overwhelming that I couldn't suck him properly. I could only keep my mouth open while he thrust in and out.

"That's it. Good girl. I knew you could do it." His voice was gravelly. "One more time. Again. While I fuck your pretty mouth."

Oh, gosh. Could I? What we were doing was super erotic—but then everything we did was erotic. It seemed to build on the last, going higher and higher. I shoved my fingers into my pussy like I did when I was alone and started grinding on them.

"Yes." Jason groaned, filling my mouth over and over. "I'm never going to get enough of you."

My orgasm combusted at the same time his did. He went still, his groans music to my ears. My body floated in bliss, enjoying the last remaining pulls of my orgasm.

He pulled the blindfold from my eyes and crawled down so he was on top of me. The moonlight shone through his patio door, illuminating the room, along with the little lamp on his nightstand. His eyes were beautiful. He was beautiful.

My heart wept. How come this would have to end someday? Couldn't it last forever?

"Yes, it has." I answered his question about whether things had changed for me. "I'm starting to develop feelings for you."

14

JASON

Did she just say that? She's developing feelings for me? Could she possibly feel what I feel? Dustin's warning that I would hurt her swirled in my mind, competing against my excitement at her admission. I knew I had feelings for her, if I were to be honest.

"Say something."

"I feel the same way, Q." I closed my eyes, trying to find a solution. When none came, I opened my eyes and turned to her. "We have to figure out what this is between us. Is it only great sex?"

"It is great sex, but it's not *only* the great sex," she said. "Is it for you?"

"No. It started that way because I knew you and I could never have a real relationship together. Christ, Quinn, I'm as old as your dad. Would you even want anything longer than this with me?" It was something that I had always worried about. She shouldn't want an old man like me.

She crawled onto me, straddling me on the bed. I loved that she'd gone out and bought her little ribbon thing. "Your age doesn't matter to me. Not at all. I mean, yeah there are some things that are different with us. I'm into technology making my life easier, and you're obviously not. I'd rather send someone a text than have to call them." She stuck out her tongue, and I laughed. "But if I didn't know how old you were, I wouldn't know how old you were. Does that make sense?" She leaned forward and kissed my nose. "Does it bother you that I'm so young?"

"I don't want to take anything away from you that you might experience as a young woman." I rubbed a hand across my face. This conversation was not heading where I wanted. "Wait. I don't mean that. I—"

Quinn laughed and pushed on my chest. "Can you stop? Why are you freaking out all of a sudden? You and I both like each other. We like what we're doing. We're exclusive on that." She bit her lip. "Otherwise, let's not worry about the future. Neither of us is promising this for the rest of our lives. No pressure. Remember?"

I blew out a deep breath, allowing my body to relax. "You're right. No pressure."

"Now. I brought you a surprise." She wiggled off me and got into her purse, which she'd set on my dresser.

"More than your strappy lingerie? How did you put that on, by the way, without getting tangled up in all those ribbons?"

She got whatever she needed out of her purse and turned. "Not gonna lie. It was tough. Took me about fifteen minutes to figure it out." She held up a tube. "But look, sir, I brought you this."

She stood next to me on the bed, and I sat up. "Get the fuck out. A Cuban cigar. Is it real?"

She laughed and pulled it out of the tube. "Of course, it's real. I know how to hook it up. I studied the ways in which to make sure it was legit, so I knew I wasn't getting ripped off." She held it up to her nose and inhaled. "I know you like them, so I wanted to surprise you."

"Let's light it."

"At your service." She handed me the supreme cigar and flicked her lighter, bringing the flame to life. She set an ashtray on the nightstand. "I came prepared."

Unbelievable. I gripped her neck and tugged her toward me, kissing her mouth. Joy spread across my chest, puffing me up a bit. "I... uh... thank you. This was so thoughtful of you." I put the cigar in my mouth and leaned forward. She lit me up and I leaned away from her, blowing out the sweet flavor. "You're making me feel like a king."

"Well, Counselor, it's only fair. You've been treating me like a queen since day one." She crawled alongside me in the bed, both of us leaning against the headboard. "You deserve the best."

I wasn't sure about that. I still hadn't been able to get used to this feeling. Happiness and guilt mixed together. Then there was the whole question of whether I deserved the best. *Shit.* For five years, I'd believed that I hadn't been enough to please Holly. Feeling like I didn't deserve the best had settled in my bones because of that. Not being the best husband had led me to wonder whether I was the best dad. Did best dads fuck their best friend's youngest daughter?

I took a drag on the cigar and passed it to Quinn. She took a small puff and passed it back. We sat that way for half the night, teasing one another and laughing about events we'd shared over the years. We'd been around one another for such a long time, it was interesting how many life experiences we shared and took for granted.

"Were you really sad about the divorce?"

"I was. But I had a recent revelation. When we were eating bananas Foster, it dawned on me that Holly and I were together because we worked well together. She was perfect for my new career as a lawyer."

"Why when we were having dessert?" she asked.

"It's you. The way you are so happy about things. Your positivity. All the stuff we do together makes me happy. I might be in control of some things, but I haven't experienced half the stuff either." I paused and tugged one of her ribbons above her breast. "When I'm with you, it's like I'm young again. Wild and carefree. I'm experiencing all of these firsts with you, and it made me realize all the things Holly and I didn't have together."

"I'm sorry. It's kinda sad."

"It is. But it's growth, right?"

Quinn nodded. "It is. I don't understand how a person finds someone that is their perfect match. Like, it will be impossible to find a man who wants the adventure like I do. Who lives and loves just as much as me. Relationships are so hard and confusing."

Something gnarly twisted in my stomach. *Impossible to find a man who wants the adventure like I do.* The thought of sharing Quinn with any man—any young guy who was her age—didn't sit well with me. "For now, let's not think about you being with anyone but me. I don't like the idea of having to share you."

I climbed on top of her and began kissing her. This next half hour, I was going to remind her that I was the man for the job, if only temporarily.

MY OFFICE DOOR FLUNG OPEN, and there stood Quinn in a red dress that went to her mid-thigh with a sassy hand on her hip. Her lips were painted red, and the urge to see how they would look wrapped around my cock was strong enough that my dick twitched. But the look on her face said I was in trouble.

"Can I help you?" I asked.

"Randall Scanberg is a client of yours?" She stepped into my office and shut the door stronger than I would have liked her to do.

"Yes. He has been. One of my better clients, actually. For about the last four years." I rolled my chair away from my desk. "Judging by the steam rolling out of your ears, I'm guessing he's not a friend of yours?"

"Does the guy actually have friends?"

"I've golfed with him a few times. So I believe he does have some. Present company included, you could say." I was hesitant to say it because Quinn was clearly about to explode. "Why don't you just spit it out? Why don't you like the guy?"

"Because he's a scumbag who preys on women." She tossed the new folder she'd made for me onto my desk. "How could you even represent a guy like him?"

"Those are some hefty allegations, Q."

"I don't give a fuck. They're accurate. Ask any female who has had to work with him at the university. It's practically a running joke there. If you had to help inside the law department, you would know the chicks all call him Randall Scumbag."

I steepled my fingers. "Has he ever been charged with sexual assault?"

"No."

"Has there been any complaints brought against him to the university?"

She folded her arms across her chest. "No."

"So no one but you and a few other women who worked there know that he's a scumbag?"

"No!" she exclaimed like she couldn't believe it.

"Candidly, if no one knows this about him and there have been no official complaints brought against him, in the eyes of the world, he is still a decent man. I can't just fire him as a client."

"Jason, you have to. He came onto me. He told me that my breasts were small, but they were still good enough for him." She rolled her eyes. "As if he was ever getting the opportunity to do anything with my breasts in the first place."

My hands were tied. I didn't like what she was revealing, but there wasn't much I could do. "Quinn, I'm sorry about that. It obviously made you feel very uncomfortable, but with zero evidence, it's out of my hands. I can't tell a long-time client, 'he's shit out of luck because my new legal clerk said you hit on her.' Especially a client that I have formed a friendship with over the years."

Smoke continued to blow out of her ears.

I stood and held up my hand in a stop gesture. "I'm sorry. But there isn't anything I can do."

"So, you're going to represent a guy who is a scumbag to women?"

It was so much more complicated than that, and obviously, any reasoning with her was moot. "He's my client. I can't *not* represent him because of something that potentially happened a few years ago."

"Potentially?" She swung her hands to her hips again. "Are you saying I'm lying?"

"No, but it's all hearsay right now, and hearsay doesn't hold up well." She was going to have to learn to calm the hell down and use her intelligence if she was going to be a good lawyer. She knew all of this, why was I suddenly having to remind her? I reached for her and placed my hands on her shoulders. "Q, chill, okay? Take a few deep breaths."

"No. The guy is a loser. That isn't the only thing he did. He rubbed against me. On purpose." She held up her hands like she was making a peace sign. "Twice."

"Why didn't you file a complaint with the school?" This was bad on so many levels, none of which were going to be in Quinn's favor. At least not right now.

"I couldn't. So many things got in the way. I wasn't going to jeopardize anything."

"What about the other girls?" I asked.

"Not sure. I think one of them did, but it never went anywhere." Quinn gave me a dirty look. "What kind of man have you become? You really need to think twice about your career and what's more important here. Doing the right thing because the guy is a scumbag or choosing money."

Zing.

She knocked my hands off her shoulders and walked out, making me feel like the biggest jerk on the planet.

Fuck.

15

QUINN

I pulled into my driveway, happy my dad wasn't home yet. What was *with* men? Jason had more than enough money to live off. He didn't need Randall Scanberg's money. *A long-time client? Golf? Disgusting.*

Anger squeezed my chest at the thought of Jason choosing that guy over me. It squeezed my chest even harder at the thought Jason had turned into one of those lawyers who let money overrun the goodness of himself. Once I got my license to practice, I was going to represent people who were good. Who did good. Who deserved help. I was going to represent the underrepresented, and money wasn't going to be an issue. I wasn't going to keep representing someone because they paid my bills—especially if I heard they did bad shit.

I wasn't going to do it. I couldn't believe Jason was. He golfed with him? Did Jason expect me to buy that as a real answer? That was a bullshit answer. Jason had more clients than he needed. He put in sixty-hour workweeks because he was so busy—what was losing one creep?

I needed a shower. I flew down the stairs and to my

bathroom, ignoring the sexy image that always came to my mind when I walked in there. Jason getting sucked off by Kimber. God, that still gave me goosebumps. So erotic. So annoying, that man.

I kicked off my heels. *We have zero evidence about this.* I tugged off my red dress. *I can't tell a long-time client he's shit out of luck because my new legal clerk said you hit on her.* I turned the water to scalding, unclasped my bra, and got rid of my panties. *Have there been any complaints brought against him to the university?* Not a single one. Why? Why hadn't I been smarter than that?

I stepped into the too-hot water and let the heat burn into my skin. I had run out of time that day. I had just finished a test. My dad had called an hour and a half before, but I'd known I had time. Mom wouldn't die without saying goodbye to me. I closed my eyes, letting the water sluice over my head. After taking my test, I'd walked into the college of law building and run into the scumbag. He'd started talking about tasks for me to do, but because of my mom, I had to get home. I'd already put her off with the test.

My sob echoed in the shower.

The shower curtain popped open, startling me. Jason stood there, worry etched into his face. I swallowed another sob, and like he wasn't dressed in a five-hundred-dollar suit, he stepped into the tub.

"I'm sorry." I couldn't hold back my sobs. Jason stepped into the stream with me and took me in his arms.

"Q, what's wrong? Why are you crying, babe?" His gentle voice and trusting comfort made me lose it.

"I wanted to file a complaint. It was the day my mom died." The words were so hard to get out, but the truth was eating me alive. "Randall came onto me. I was already late." *Hiccup.* "She was dying. I'd hurried and taken my test."

"Shh." Jason's big arms wrapped tight around my naked body. "You don't have to tell me now."

"I do. He got behind me and rubbed against my ass. Like really rubbed."

"The way I rub against your ass," Jason filled in.

"Yeah, exactly like that. And he was..." I choked. *I can do this.* "He was hard. He did it again. I bolted, and as I ran down the hallway, I passed the admin office. I knew I should go in right away."

"But your mom." Jason leaned forward and shut off the water. "Keep going. Tell me everything."

"I thought it might take a minute. How long could it take to tell someone you got groped without consent?" My entire chest was trembling. My legs shaking. "I pushed the door open. I told the student helper I was there to file a formal complaint, and it took her forever to find the proper paperwork. Once she laid it on the counter..." The night-mare settled heavily in my chest. *Quinn, where are you?* My sister had called the second I'd picked up the pen.

Jason carried me out of the shower and had enough foresight to grab a few towels from the closet. He set me on my bed and wrapped me up. His clothes were ruined. "I missed it." The sobs were back. "Elizabeth called me. 'Dad is calling her time of death, Quinn. Where the hell are you?' I dropped the pen and paper and left. I went home. After helping take care of my mom the whole time she was sick, I wasn't there when she needed me the most. I failed her. Over something stupid."

Jason started peeling out of his wet socks, his pants, and his tie. "It doesn't sound like it was something stupid." Off went his shirt.

"But it was, don't you see? I missed her death. I missed..." I swallowed, letting the tears fall. "I missed my mom because of Professor Scanberg." My entire body shook. My teeth chattered.

Jason was completely naked standing in my room now. His clothes were in a heap on the carpet. It suddenly occurred to me what the fuck kind of situation we were in. I jumped off the bed. "My dad. Oh my God, my dad is going to find you here. Get dressed. Get dressed. Who knows when he'll get here?"

Jason stood in front of me, his hand out. "Q, relax. It's Tuesday night. Doesn't he bowl on Tuesdays?"

All the air got sucked out of my body the way a wave retreated from land. It was Tuesday. "I—I'm, oh. My gosh."

Jason sat on the edge of my bed, pulling me into his lap. "You're a wreck. You're starting to worry me. Take a few deep breaths." He rubbed my back in slow circles. "So afterward, you never went back, I take it."

I shook my head. "It had been busy and was no longer a big deal. You guys and all of our extended family were around. Then the funeral." I shrugged. "It wasn't like he raped me, anyway. By the time the funeral was over, I was drained. I was so angry with myself, like how could I have let that happen? What did I do that gave him the idea that he could touch me like that?"

Jason stayed silent, letting me vent about something I'd never mentioned to anyone.

I raised my shoulders. "But I'm sure other women have had worse things happen to them, so there was no point in going back. My mom was probably so disappointed in me for not being there with her."

"For what it's worth, I don't think Debra would be at all disappointed in you for standing up to a perv like Scanberg." Jason chuckled. "She never told you about the time she made your dad and me march with her on the steps of the Capitol for women's rights?"

I wiped my eyes. "What?"

"Your mom was a big advocate for women everything. You know."

I nodded. She was a feminist in her own time. A feminist right when it was becoming something to talk about.

Jason squeezed my thigh. "In college, one of her professors pissed her off because he showed some film that had women catering to men. I don't remember. They were waitresses or something, wearing bikinis. It was this beach thing. The movie has probably been banned at this point. But yeah, guys were groping the waitresses, and the way your mom always told it was that she stood up in the middle of class and called the professor an egotistical cocksucker."

I laughed. "Really? I've never heard this."

"Oh yeah. Got all the women to walk out of class. Anyway, afterward, she formed a civil rights movement, as she coined it. Your dad and I teased her incessantly about it. We never believed getting thirty people to show up at the Capitol to protest the importance of women's rights would change the world."

I bounced in his lap. I could feel a *but* in there. "You were wrong."

Jason nodded. "We were wrong. The news estimated that five thousand people showed up that day, and it was all because of your mom."

I clapped, squealing loudly. My mom was so cool.

He smiled too, probably thinking of all the good times he'd shared with my parents. "So, like I said before, I don't think Debra was worried about you not being there at the time of her death. She knows what you were doing, Quinn."

It was more important now that I should have finished

what I'd started with Scanberg. But I could only do so much because I wasn't a licensed lawyer yet. The weight of the world lifted off my shoulders.

Jason kissed my forehead.

"Thank you for telling me this. Thank you for coming to find me after I was so mean to you." I kissed his cheek. His stubble was prickly against my lips. "I'm sorry I said that about your career and money." I was ashamed I'd thrown such cruel words at him.

He lifted my chin so I was eye-to-eye with him. "Don't be. You're right. You'll figure out that you can't always work for free. But we have to come to some understanding. I have to figure out a way to get rid of the guy without hurling accusations that can't be proven. I can't get sued for libel."

"I understand. We'll come up with something."

"This whole time you carried that burden with you about your mom, and if I had known—or your dad—we could have set you straight sooner. I know it still sucks that you weren't there when she passed, but the blow wouldn't have been as rough for you had you known this."

"I was so ashamed of myself. So angry. I didn't want to tell anyone. They were already judging me anyway that my test had to come first. Let alone the rest of it." I bit my lip to stop it from quivering. "Plus, if I had done exactly that, Scanberg would have never been able to do that to me."

"No. Your actions have nothing to do with his. It seems that a man like him would have done that at any time—any chance he had." Jason shook his head. "Don't be ashamed. Everyone makes mistakes and choices. Even when we know death is near, like we did with Debra, we still don't know when. You wouldn't have known. You could have missed your test and gone home, and it could have happened hours later." He raised his brows. "Or Scanberg could have cornered you the next day."

"You're right. I'll always feel bad. But now that I know about her and the Capitol, I have a lot more faith that she was proud of me for doing what I was doing."

"Exactly." Jason glanced at his watch. "It's getting late. I definitely cannot be here in wet clothes when Greg gets home."

"No. That would be awful."

I stood and watched Jason struggle to put on his wet pants. "Here. Let me get you some of my dad's shorts and a shirt to put on. You can't put that stuff back on."

I quickly got Jason some things. I hoped like hell my dad wouldn't miss the clothes and went back to my room. "Here you go. Thanks for being here."

"I'm always here for you when you need someone to talk to, okay?"

"Okay." I got on my tiptoes and kissed him goodbye. "Text me later?"

"Always. And we'll figure something out for Scanberg. I promise."

I believed him. I wasn't sure what, but we would be able to figure something out.

16

JASON

It had been two weeks since the night in Quinn's bathroom. I could tell that our talk had lifted a burden off her shoulders. Every fucking day I thought about my client and what I could do to pawn him off to another associate, but nothing seemed to pan out quite well enough to follow through with.

Quinn and I had tossed around some ideas from telling him the truth to lying to him about my caseload. Plus, I was knee-deep in shit, so there were days when that was literally the last thing on my mind before I went to bed at night. That and Quinn.

I closed up the office and slid into my car. My phone buzzed with a text.

Quinn: *Should I head over now?*

Me: *I'll meet you there.*

When I pulled in, Quinn was safely in my garage, waiting for me.

"Hey, babe." I kissed her lips.

"'Hey, babe' back. I brought you something." She pushed open her door and retrieved a wine bag. "Bourbon." She held it up out of the bag. "Not sure who they are, but the clerk assured me this brand was rising on the popularity charts."

"Wow. Thank you. Let's go in and try some."

I poured us both a glass, and we sat together on the couch in our usual position. Me in my corner and she hogging up the rest of the couch, her feet in my lap. "I like our little cocoon we've built."

"Me too." I took a sip of the bourbon. It went down smooth. "This is good. Thank you."

"You're welcome." She took a sip, set her glass on the end table, then crawled up into my lap so she was straddling me. My semi-wood settled nicely in the crease of her ass. I could tell there was something on her mind.

"What are you thinking about, Q? Spit it out."

She blushed. "What makes the anal thing so intriguing to you?"

She might not want it, but I wanted us to be in a place where we could talk about it all, so I took a deep breath and let my heart do the talking. "It's forbidden. There's an element of wildness to it." I peered at her—she was intrigued. "You've never tried it with anyone?"

She shook her head. "Never. It doesn't seem like a place that would feel good."

"Maybe not. But there are people who enjoy it. I've not been on the receiving end, so I don't have any experience with that."

She kissed me. Small little pecks one right after another, over and over, put an end to our conversation.

"What's this for?" I mumbled between kisses.

"I have lots of feelings for you." She let out a sigh. "We look great together." She pointed to the windows, where our reflection was highlighted in color. The sky was dark.

I couldn't disagree with her. We looked amazing together. She fit in my arms perfectly. Everything about her fit nicely. My hand along the curve of her hip and stomach. The way her ass fit perfectly snug against my dick. Christ, even the way her head met my face—my lips hitting the perfect spot on the back of her head. I inhaled the sweet scent of her hair.

"I have lots of feelings for you too, Q."

I was scared as fuck that there was nothing either one of us could do about them.

I WATCHED Randall Scanberg pull into my parking lot from my office window. I'd strategically planned something for Quinn to do outside of the office. I had no intentions of making her feel uncomfortable by running into the guy. Until I could figure something out, I would keep her far away from him.

A few minutes later, he sauntered into my office. His hair was whiteout gray, and he'd lost a few pounds since the last time I'd seen him. Must not have been indulging in dinners at the country club.

"How are you doing?"

"Randall is doing pretty good. Moving a little slower these days." Randall always referred to himself in the third person. Always.

"That's what happens when you age. What are you pushing these days? Fifty-eight?" I moved a chair over, motioning for him to sit.

"No, Randall is lucky number sixty-nine."

I clenched my jaw. A comment like that wouldn't have

bothered me before. "Almost seventy. I wouldn't have guessed that."

"Randall can't believe it either. His golf game has gotten better, though."

"That's some good news if I've ever heard." I took his newly revised will out of the folder on my desk. I wanted to make this as quick as possible. I should have told Quinn to take the afternoon off. "Here is the latest version. Let's go over it one last time and make sure everything is as it should be, and I can have Leona come and be a witness."

I went over all the changes he'd asked me to make. He was a little off his game this time. When was the last time I'd seen him? Four months ago? Five? While I showed him the additions of the two commercial properties he'd purchased and wanted to make damn sure that his estranged youngest son, Tony, didn't have access to them, I watched him. His cheeks were sallow. Even his normally red-tinged skin looked a little pale.

"You're looking at Randall like you know he is sick."

I locked eyes with him. "You're sick?"

"Cancer. Damn, Randall thought he could live forever since he's already outlived four wives and a daughter."

"How bad?" I would never wish cancer on anyone. Not after what we'd gone through with Debra.

"Stage IV lung cancer. Which is why Randall needed to get that will updated. Did you add in the part about Muffy and Millie?"

The cats. I flipped through the pages. "I did. I forgot to cover that with you. Millie and Muffy will be given to Roderick Scanberg. If Roderick is unable to take the cats for any reason, they will be given to your sister, Bessy."

"You sure you won't take the cats? Do you good to have a little pussy in your life."

I didn't acknowledge the *pussy* part of his comment. "I don't know what led you to believe I was good with cats, but I can assure you that if I inherited them, they would likely die in my care. Bessy is a good choice." I couldn't even keep plants alive, and they only required sunlight and water. The burden of working too much.

Randall waved me away with a hand. "Randall is ready to sign."

I made a few more copies and buzzed Leona. She came in right away, and we managed to get his new will signed. "Thanks, Leona."

"Sure thing."

Randall and I stood, and I walked him to my door. "Here you go." I handed him a folder with one of his copies. "I'm sorry to hear about the cancer. You doing chemo and all that?"

"Nope. Shit's worse for you than smoking."

"You might change your mind about that when you start feeling the effects of the cancer."

Randall waved me away once more and trotted down the hall. Just as I was closing my door, I heard Quinn. "Professor Scanberg."

Christ. I flung open my door ready to intervene.

"You are?" Randall asked.

"Quinn Brenning. I was at the university. Law school. Worked in your department." There was an edge to Quinn's voice, and even though he likely deserved jail time for his groping stints, I didn't want her to go too hard on him since he was, in fact, dying.

"There were a lot of kids worked in that department. If you'll excuse me." He obviously didn't give a rat's ass who she was.

"Actually, no. I won't excuse you. I did that before. You

know you groped me in college? Twice." Quinn's voice was firm and unwavering.

I desperately wanted to step out into the hallway, but Quinn was handling it.

"Those are some hefty allegations, young lady."

"You know what? I think you do remember me, and you've probably sexually harassed so many females in your department that you're playing dumb. Easier to pretend you don't remember than to deal with any potential consequences."

"You don't know what you're talking about." Scanberg's voice was low, condescending. "What are you? First-year attorney? This your second year? No one will believe you. Go away, little kid."

"No. Admit you remember who I am."

My heart was racing. With pride. With anger. With all sorts of shit. I was so proud of her for finding the courage to say something, even if he was being an ass, but Quinn had likely expected that to happen. It wasn't every day someone freely admitted to sexual harassment allegations.

"You know what? Come to think of it, Randall does remember you. You're the little girl with the little useless boobs. Looks like some things haven't changed."

I flew through my door and met them in the hallway. I caught her right as she was about to plow into me.

"You know what that motherfucker just told me?" Her cheeks were on fire. Her chest was beet red.

"I heard all of it." I glanced at Randall. "I'm glad we got your inheritance from your parents figured out this last year and now your will is done." I tried to keep my anger in check. "You're not welcome here anymore. You're going to have to take your future requests elsewhere." I clenched my jaw. "Leave. Now."

"You're going to let this kid ruin our friendship over a lie?"

I glanced at Quinn. Her chest heaved up and down. Her eyes were wide. "I am. She's my employee, and this is a huge problem. I'm not going to allow my employees to be treated the way you just treated her."

"Bullshit. You'll be lucky if I pay your bill." Randall waved his file folder and walked off, leaving Quinn and me standing alone in the hall.

"I'm sorry. I tried to schedule you away from the office so you wouldn't have an encounter with him."

"He's a dirtbag. Scum. But you know what the joke is on him." Her hands were trembling.

I nodded. "The joke is on him. He has stage IV lung cancer. That's likely the last time I'll ever see him again."

"That sucks. I hate cancer." She gave me her little rebellious smirk. "But no. You know what I'm doing? Starting two days ago?"

Oh, God. I cringed. "What?"

"Making a list of all the females I went to law school with. Professor Scanberg is going to be my first official case once I get my license. I'm reaching out to all the women in my year and the year below me. Surely, someone has documents or proof that he's touched them inappropriately or said something inappropriate after all this time. Clearly, he's still a pompous ass who thinks he can get away with this."

I cupped her cheeks and kissed the fuck out of her. She was the most amazing, fearless woman I had ever met. I pulled back, breathless. "What do you need me to do to help you?"

17

QUINN

I took the last few steps to the law department. My veins were literally on fire. I was on fire. I couldn't sit still. I had contacted five women from college—all of whom remembered Scanberg. And all of them had admitted he'd done something shady to them in some form. Unfortunately, not one of them had any actual evidence.

When I had free time at the office, I was working on this. I was researching old emails that I had gotten from previous classes. I was scouring old schedules I'd taken pictures of on my phone. Anything I had that could possibly lead me to more women.

The search turned up absolutely nothing. The building that I used to work in hadn't changed. It was still the ugly gray-and-white building with columns that made it look like it belonged in Paris or Berlin rather than in downtown Denver. It felt weird—but good—to be standing here. There had to be something on Scanberg. Somewhere.

The door handle was cold against my fingers when I pulled it open. I stepped inside. Yeah, I pretty much felt like

I was heading back to Pretrial Litigations or something. My heels clicked on the tile with purpose. Randall Scanberg had retired two years ago. Surely, there were still students in school who had dealt with him.

My phone buzzed with a text.

Jason: *Find anything?*

Me: *Nothing. But there is a class that gets out in like five minutes. Going to ask any of the females if they know anything.*

Jason: *Good luck, babe.*

I sent Jason a heart. His support was unreal. I loved that man.

Oh, wait. I do? I loved him. *Did I just think that?* I'd always loved him. But this was feeling a little different than that love. This was feeling like I boyfriend-loved him. Not like I family-loved him. Well, I was in trouble, wasn't I? I considered all the dirty sex. I loved that. But I also was *in love* with him. The way he smiled when he was teasing me. The way his face lit up when I brought him a chai latte or some other drink of the week I thought he should try. How comfortable it was for us to talk about work and his kids. My life was easy with him. We could fuck like rabbits or chill and watch a movie. He understood me. My mistakes. My successes. My potential.

The question was whether Jason would be okay taking our relationship public? Would he be ashamed of me when Cera learned we were a couple? Or what about Holly?

Students started pouring out of class, and it took me a second to catch my bearings, putting Jason out of my mind.

"Um, excuse me?" I stepped in front of a random girl. "Hi. I'm Quinn Brenning. I was a law student here. Did you ever have Professor Scanberg as a teacher?"

The girl shook her head. "No, sorry."

I did this to five more girls, but everyone I asked said no. The lecture hall was cleared out. Two girls were walking together, and both looked at me expectantly. I felt it in before I'd even asked. One of these girls knew Professor Scanberg. "Hi. I'm Quinn Brenning. I went to school here." I went into my whole monologue about the professor. Both girls glanced at each other.

"Actually, we do. We had him as freshman. Both of us."

Oh, thank goodness. I tried to conceal my excitement. I had to word this properly. After all, I didn't want to lead them. "Did either of you, ah, ever have any complaints about him?"

The short blonde laughed. "Who didn't?"

"He was bad news. Both of us complained to the university, but no one listened."

"What did he do?" I glanced down the hallway, uncertain whether we should have this conversation here.

"Oh, he tried hitting on me all the time. Thank God that was all he did."

"I wasn't so lucky."

Goosebumps covered my arms. I was failing at this. *Should I introduce myself? Should I tell them where I work?* I cleared my throat. "Look. I'm putting together names of women he mistreated or sexually harassed or abused. More than once, he did something physical to me—nothing like rape or anything—but there are more women out there. It sounds like both of you have some information. Could we exchange names and phone numbers? Would you two be willing to give an account of your experiences with him?"

The taller girl looked away and back at her friend.

I was losing her. "Please. He needs to be held accountable in the eyes of the law."

"I heard he already died."

"He's still alive. He's not a professor. But if we can pull enough evidence together, I can take it to the police, and with enough evidence, they can take it to the DA to indict him. Which is what should happen. It should have happened a long time ago." I spoke with authority. I had to get these women to pursue this with me. "Especially if you filed a complaint. Do you guys have a break? We could go have lunch and talk about all of this."

I held my breath as both of the girls spoke to each other. Finally, they turned to me. "We would love that."

I STRADDLED Jason on his couch. The sun was starting to settle on the horizon, and I could almost see our reflection in his windows perfectly. This was the best seat in the house.

"The one girl has a video."

"What's on the video?" Jason asked.

It was always so hard to think when I was around this man. His voice was pure honey. His eyes were a devastating green this evening. And he'd forgotten to shave this morning, so his stubble was already turning into facial hair. My fingers had a whole mind of their own as they smoothed across his skin. "I love when you don't shave."

"Hey. Focus, woman. You're going to get me hard, and then you know what's going to happen."

I grinned. "How do you expect me to focus with dick talk?"

He chuckled. "Dick talk? You're hilarious. And once we have this conversation, I'll gladly give you all the dick you want to talk about."

"Fine. I'll be quick. The video shows Scanberg sliding against Kayla Champer like he did to me. Plus, she had it going so long that she also filmed him—" I fake gagged. "Jacking off behind her when she was at the desk."

Jason's jaw tensed. "And all of this is on video? Why the hell hasn't anyone done anything?"

"Well, apparently the girl tried. But someone in the department threatened her scholarship. She has zero money. No dad. Just her and her mom, and her mom works nights doing unconventional mom jobs—"

"What the fuck does that mean? She a drug dealer?"

"No. Stripper. Anyway, when that happened, Kayla backed off. She couldn't afford to jeopardize anything." I continued brushing my fingertips along Jason's jawline. "The other girl, Cassie Moser, was the one that he made dirty comments to, and she has no real evidence."

Jason stared into space for a long time before he met my gaze. "What are you going to do, Q? You know this is going to involve whoever is covering the fact that they had a potential scandal on their hands. It's likely Scanberg and the head of the department. Maybe more."

"Not sure. Haven't thought that far ahead. All I've thought about is getting enough women to speak and admit that they were a victim. He deserves to pay for this. At the very least, something that makes sure he can't ever do it again."

"He does have cancer. You know he'll die from it. He's not seeking treatment."

Jason's words hung thick in the air. He was right. But death didn't excuse this. My stomach tightened. "I owe it to these girls to know that someone cares about them. That someone has walked in their shoes and that every single one of us has a voice and we are important enough. We matter. Not to mention that someone in that department is covering up stuff big time. That might be worse."

Jason was nodding. "You're gonna have your work cut out for you."

I clapped. "I know. It's exciting." I kissed the corner of his lip. "Now, how about that dick talk?"

"What do you want to talk about?" He kissed me back.

"About how much I like making you happy. Come on." I stood, and Jason had zero choice but to follow. I pulled out my phone and found a porn site. When his chuckle vibrated against my back, I giggled. "Just one more thing I've been wanting to experience with you. Might as well cross it off while we're at it."

We sat at the edge of his bed and proceeded to watch the story of a woman selling real estate. It was a large, beautiful empty house, and of course, the guy who came to look at the property was muscular, wearing a button-down shirt that was unbuttoned. The real estate agent was dressed equally sexy in a short miniskirt, was probably pantyless, and her nipples protruded through the fabric of her white top. "This never happens in real life."

"Never," Jason agreed.

We watched the two of them make the rounds, and of course, the man followed her up the stairs, eyeing her ass the whole way.

"I didn't think she was wearing panties," I said when the camera zoomed in on her. "He's waiting for the perfect moment."

"It'll be the balcony."

Sure enough, a minute later, the two of them were going at it on the balcony. Her boobs were exposed, lifted over the glass railing, and the guy was fucking her from behind. I squeezed my thighs together, loving the way she looked. So perfect. So pristine. So classy but dirty. I got onto my knees between Jason's legs.

The way he watched me was something out of a freaking movie. It was like he was enthralled with me and couldn't wait to watch my next move. I felt cherished when he looked at me so deeply. It was almost like his feelings mirrored my own. I shivered.

I unzipped his pants and pulled out his cock. Behind me, my phone made porn-y sounds of skin slapping and mixed groans of approval. I took him into my mouth as far as he could go. In and out. This turned me on as much as it did him. I circled my tongue around his tip, loving the feel of how hard yet soft he was.

"So, I'm going to watch this while you suck my dick? I have a better idea. How about I go down on you while you watch." He hauled me up and basically threw me on the bed, taking zero time to undress me. His tongue went up one side of my leg, then he started on the other leg, never reaching his intended spot. The video was now showing another couple coming into the same house, thinking it was empty. They started having sex on the living room floor, and I was so ready for Jason to take me in his mouth.

A hot breath of air tickled my clitoris. I shivered.

"Lick me. Touch me. Do something." I touched my throbbing clit, and Jason pushed my hand away.

"Not yet." He sucked on the skin all around the place I needed it the most. Sweat beaded against my forehead and breasts. I was so close to coming. "I want you to come like this. It's a fucking wonder how you can come without direct contact." His voice was low and gruff.

"Don't stop. I'm about to. I just need—" Darkness lined

my vision, and stars exploded. My entire body shook as my orgasm took hold of me.

His mouth latched on to my clit, and I screamed at the delicate touch. "Oh my gosh. That is so... so sensitive."

He raised his head and chuckled. "I have another idea. Let's shower."

In the shower, neither of us spoke. I took the soap and washed his back and chest, admiring all the contours of his muscles. I loved his chest hair and nipples, biting each one before I soaped them up. Then it was my turn, and Jason took great care of me, washing me in return. He shampooed my hair, giving my scalp some extra rubbing attention like a salon would.

"I love the way you make me feel, Jason." I swallowed. I could get these words out. "A small part of me thinks I'll be let down because that's how my past encounters with guys have been. But every single time we're together, it's perfect."

He chuckled. "Yeah, it is perfect." He shut off the shower and offered me a towel. "And I love the way you make me feel too." He kissed my shoulder blade. "Spend the night with me?"

I swallowed. This was a big milestone for us. Not the spending the night thing. I wasn't sure whether it was all the sex or the gentle motions in the shower, but something much deeper than words happened between us. I could see it in his eyes. I felt like my eyes were showing him the same thing. Perhaps it was the trust being built between us. I nodded. "I would love to."

That night, being in Jason's arms was a different experience for me. It suddenly felt like my life was on the right track. Between him and getting closer to obtaining my bar exam results as well as knowing I would be giving those women some comfort if everything went right, my life was starting to take a big turn for better things to come.

And somehow, I had the man lying next to me to thank for his support, especially for the growth of who I'd become. Or perhaps, I'd always been there, but he was now bringing her to the surface.

18

JASON

I paced my office. Dustin had nailed it. I was falling in love with Quinn. I wasn't falling so much as I had already fallen. How had it happened so quickly? Who was I kidding? It hadn't been quick. It was spread out over a lifetime, and the past nine weeks had been the icing on the cake.

We needed to tell her dad about our relationship. If I wanted any chance of a real relationship with her—one that was the opposite of what I'd believed to be real with Holly— then we needed to start. Sneaking around was fun. It intensified the pleasure. But at my age, I wanted to do something I hadn't done in ages, maybe never. I wanted to start living.

I wanted to go on more dates. I wanted to be in public with Quinn. I wanted people to see how proud I was of her. I wanted to bring her over to her dad's monthly business parties and take her home with me. I wanted to shoot the shit with her as my date. And I didn't want to hide anymore. It was time.

Me: *Do you have a second?*

Quinn: *Yep. Just putting more books on my shelves.*

Me: *Aren't those shelves full by now?*

Quinn: *Close. But not quite.*

Seconds later, my door opened, and Quinn stepped inside. She had on a billowy knee-length black skirt and a pink blouse. The image she presented actually made me chuckle. I took great joy in knowing what she was like beneath the image she presented. Was she wearing panties today? My dick jumped just thinking about it.

"You look nice."

"Thank you. As do you. What can I do for you?"

I steepled my fingers. "I don't want to do this anymore."

Her shoulders sagged. She glanced around my office then back to me. She took a slow step forward. "Why?"

"Not *us* this. In secret. I want more, Quinn."

"What do you mean?"

"We need to tell your dad." I closed one eye and studied her.

She looked serious like she didn't understand.

Should I tell her I'm in love with her? We were both used to skirting around our relationship having any deeper meaning, but enough was enough. I was hungry for life. With her.

"I don't want to tell my dad. He'll ruin this."

I shook my head. "He won't. He can't ruin what's between us. No one can."

"Well, assuming my dad begrudgingly accepts this, everyone will still think I'm not standing on my own merit. They'll think I'm riding your coat tails because we're sleeping together."

"That's not true. Plus, when have you ever cared about what anyone thinks?"

"I care about this. This is my career. I'm working on this thing with Scanberg and all the women. No, Jason.

Everyone will think I'm only working here because we're a couple."

Her face was flushed, but she was dead serious. How had I not anticipated that she would think this? I stood. "What are you saying, Quinn? You don't want a relationship with me?" Anger coursed through my bloodstream. "That I'm good enough for fucking and experimenting, for taking your sexual pleasures to the next level, but I'm not good enough to be your man in public?"

She was already shaking her head. "No. That's not what I'm saying at all." She chewed on her bottom lip. "I'm only saying that I'm young. Our clients, our friends—probably Cera and my sister—they won't think I got this job because I can do it. No one will think you've hired me because I have potential or that I'm intelligent or anything like that. They'll think you were obligated because of the sex. That you were obligated because of who I am to you."

My chest was full of anger. How could she be saying this? After everything? "Isn't that the partial truth? I wasn't obligated. Trust me, I could have filled that room with much more qualified candidates than you. But you are here because of who you are. You wanted to be here. What happened to wanting to learn from the best? That night at your house when you knew I had an empty office and Greg pushed you to talk to me—that was a favor I wouldn't have done for anyone."

She stepped back like I'd slapped her. She put a hand on her hip. Oh, that had made her mad. There was steam coming from her ears again. I shook my head. This was not how I'd imagined this conversation would go.

"So you don't think I'm smart enough to be your partner? You don't think I could have made it here without your help?"

"You're twisting my words around. You're wrong. It's like you're pressing for a fight."

"Really? Did you or did you not just say that I'm only here because you did a favor for me?" She put a hand to her waist.

"Quinn—"

"Answer the question, Counselor."

"Yes, but—"

She threw her hands up. "Unbelievable. You're a fucking tool. Did you already anticipate that we would fall into bed too? Wow. Why not hire Quinn so I could get a side of ass too?"

"Knock it off. I didn't fucking say that."

"Yes, you did," she screamed at me.

"Lower your voice." I stepped toward her.

"Make me."

I did the only thing I could think of to that smart mouth of hers. I kissed her. Full throttle. Pushed her back against the wall of my office and kissed the fucking sass out of her. Her hands were everywhere at first, pushing me away, but then they were digging into my forearms, pulling me closer, messing up my hair, and biting into my shoulders with greed.

My hands traveled down her front and up her skirt between her thighs. She was soaked. I pulled back. Both of us were breathing hard. My cock strained against my trousers. I flicked my belt open and unzipped my pants. "You better fucking tell me no right now if this isn't what you want."

She turned her head to the open door. This was so fucking risky. My chest was caught in my throat. I could hardly swallow. Was it bad that I wanted her like this? Anger still filtered through me.

"I'm so mad at you, I could scream," she said, her voice likely carrying out of my office.

"I'm two seconds away from covering your mouth with my hand." I spread her thighs apart with my knee. "And another two from pounding into you," I whispered.

"Do it," she sassed. "What are you waiting for?" Her attitude would have broken a smaller man. I covered her mouth with my hand and slid into her wet heat, elevating her enough to pin her against the wall.

"You. Are. Wrong." I pounded into her hard. Not sorry. "So. Fucking. Wrong."

She moaned into my hand, squeezing my hips with her thighs, gripping my forearms so hard, it felt like the skin was breaking.

"I love you for so many things that you are." Harder and harder into her. "None of which have anything to do with obligation or fucking being nice because you're my best friend's daughter."

Her eyes clenched shut, and her pussy convulsed around my cock. "That's right. Come all over my big dick." I was relentless pounding into her so hard, the frame of my diploma was thunking against the wall with every thrust. But I didn't stop. "You. Fucking. Hear. Me. Q? I'm. In. Love. With. You." My cock swelled to epic proportions. My thighs burned from drilling into her so hard. "It's more than obligation." I unloaded into her. My hand fell from her mouth.

My chest heaved. I shook. I nudged Quinn's cheek so she would look at me. Her eyes blazed. I wasn't sure at this point whether it was anger or arousal. Maybe both. "Christ, did I hurt you?"

She was already shaking her head. "No."

"Quinn?" The unmistakable question in Greg's voice

had me pulling out of and away from Quinn while she scrambled to fix her panties and skirt. I wiped the sweat from my forehead and buckled up my pants.

"Dad?" Quinn's high-pitched squeal echoed through the room.

"I can't believe this." His voice was pure shock. Not anger. Not yet. "You guys are sleeping together."

With my pants back on, I turned around to face hell. Greg's eyebrows were cinched in surprise. I reached behind Quinn and shut my office door, waiting for an explosion. He was acting way too calm for a man who'd caught his best friend fucking his youngest daughter.

"Dad, it's not what it looks like."

Greg raised an eyebrow at me, not daring to take his eyes off me, even though Quinn was trying to talk. "It sure as hell better be what it looks like. Otherwise, I'm calling the police."

I cleared my throat. "No. This was consensual. This wasn't the first time we've done this." There was absolutely no liquid in my throat. Quinn's gaze was solemn. I couldn't fucking read her mind. Greg was eerily unperturbed. "What I mean is that—"

"Dad, Jason and I have been seeing each other for like two months. In secret. We were afraid to tell you. Afraid that you would freak out."

"I would have to say, I'm pretty freaked out. How in the hell could something like this have happened?" He rubbed his forehead. "I've trusted you with my life. My family. My wife. The girls. How could you start something like this?"

"It just happened. Quinn and I—"

"Dad, I started this with Jason. He tried to stop it. He tried to tell me no. I wouldn't take no for an answer. Me. Dad, look at me." Quinn reached for Greg and managed to turn him so that he was looking at Quinn and not staring me down like he wanted to use a scalpel on my eye. "I'm in love with him."

This was not how I'd imagined either of us professing our love to each other. Greg would call bullshit.

"You're twenty-six. Where did I go wrong with you?" Greg looked at me, pity in his eyes. "Are you really trying to trick her into thinking she needs someone like you? She has her whole life ahead of her."

He had every right to be angry about this, and I tried not to focus too much on his *someone like me* comment. "I'm not tricking her. She's a grown woman." I omitted the voice in my head that was saying I hoped she needed someone like me because I needed her. He wasn't ready to hear that. When he was less shocked and mad, I would have to tell him. Because I wanted Quinn more than anything else.

"She's twenty-six."

"I'm twenty-six." Frustration laced Quinn's voice. "Old enough to know what I'm doing. Give me credit."

"I can't even think right now." He pointed a finger at me. "I would have never done this to you. You're too old for her."

"I know." I was. I struggled with this myself.

"You know? But it's not stopping you from touching her." He gestured to the wall.

"It's not that easy."

"Make this easy for me, then." Greg squeezed the bridge of his nose. "How in the hell can this be my life?"

I'd been asking myself that same question for almost nine weeks. I was at a loss for words. He was right on all accounts. I wasn't the right guy for Quinn. She was younger, sexier, and smarter. She had her whole life ahead of her. There were young dudes out there who could keep up with her if she wanted to do a couple's triathlon, whereas I was debatable because of my age. *Shit. Fuck that. I could totally keep up with her.*

"Dad, I'm sorry you found out like this. Walking in on us having..." Her voice drifted off.

"See? You can't even say the word, and you really think I should understand this arrangement?"

Her rebel look came out, and she put a hand to her hip. *Oh God.*

"Sex. Sex. Sex. You walked in while he was fucking my brains out." Her voice was rising with every word.

I was shaking my head. *Please don't do this.*

"In fact, we were having our first real argument. Angry sex. It was an angry fuck, and I enjoyed every minute of it."

"Quinn," I pleaded. I closed my eyes, wishing I was anywhere but in this room with my best friend and his daughter. "Stop. Please. Your dad doesn't need details about this..." *This angry sex.*

"It makes me sick thinking about you touching her. All the times you've been around us with Quinn being a minor—"

"Dad—"

"Stop, Greg. Don't even fucking say that or imply any sickening shit, man." My anger rose at what he hadn't said. "This just started between us. This crazy attraction. So we acted on it."

"Look, Dad. You have two options because I'm not stopping this. Jason and I have an amazing relationship. When I said that I'm in love with him, I meant it. He is by far the best thing that has ever happened to me. He treats me great. He respects me and my opinions." She glanced at me. "He believes in me. He is everything I want in someone. So what if he's twenty years older than I am? If we didn't know, we wouldn't know."

Quinn folded her arms over her chest, and I squelched down the urge to hug her. I felt all of those same things about her.

Greg sighed as if he'd given up. "We can talk about this whenever you come home."

"Wait." I stopped Greg from walking away. "What did you come here for?" I couldn't think of any legal matters that he'd asked me to do or any reason why he would have stopped by.

"I came to talk to my friend about a woman I met. Came to see whether you wanted to go grab a drink or something. But I'm definitely not feeling that now. Not to mention the fact if I would still even call you my friend." Greg stalked out of my office.

Why did I have to go and have angry sex? Greg hadn't dated since Debra died. If he'd met someone, it was obviously important enough for him to come and talk, and here I was, fucking his daughter.

Quinn tapped me on the shoulder and came into my arms. "We'll work this out. I promise."

"Did he say he met a woman?" I asked.

"He did. But I wasn't in any position to ask for an explanation, so I ignored it."

"Where in the hell did he meet someone at?"

Quinn shrugged. "Not sure. But there you go. You got your wish of telling my dad about us."

"I wouldn't call it a wish, but it was time. Don't you get it? I'm old. Fuck, in three and a half years, I'll be fifty. I don't want to hide the only amazing thing I have going on in my life. I want to embrace it."

"You said you loved me," she said.

"I meant it. You told your dad you loved me."

"I meant it."

"Good."

"Good."

"Then get back to work."

"Fine." She moved to the door then turned to me, a large smile on her face. "That was fucking intense." She nodded to the wall. "Feel free to do that next time we fight."

Laughter and calmness floated through my chest as she dragged my door shut behind her.

Christ. Who am I these days? What kind of man have I turned into? Quinn had me flipped up and down and spun sideways. I had turned into a crazy man. She made me lose control. Over and over.

Was I going through a midlife crisis? Because knowing the potential loss of my friendship with Greg still wasn't enough to make me regret what was happening. At forty-six years old, I was finally living out my own sexual desires, experiencing all of these firsts that I should have been doing when Holly and I had first gotten married.

It was evident that there was one thing I needed. That was to grab on to this new me and hold on for the wild ride —despite how badly my friend was going to hate it.

19

QUINN

The shower water fell across my body, making fast rivulets down my stomach and legs. Memories of Jason stepping in here with his clothes on flooded my mind. He loved me. He was in love with me. I'd always imagined that when the man of my dreams told me he's in love with me, it would start at a fancy place for dinner, where he would talk about his dreams for the future and how he wanted me to be a part of that future. He would tell me he loved me and wanted to spend the rest of his life with me. That would be followed up by roses and champagne.

Not once in my life had I ever imagined I would be getting fucked into oblivion while I was angry as sin with the man I was in love with... and enjoy it. Angry sex.

Oh my gosh. It replayed in my mind over and over. *You. Fucking. Hear. Me. Q. I'm. In. Love. With. You.*

I needed to think. I could never think when he was around, consuming all of my thoughts. I had to sort out the reality of our situation. Was I really that worried about people finding out we're a couple because I thought they would judge me and question how I got in his office?

I shut off the shower. I dried off and smoothed my fingers across the small love bite on my breast. This relationship didn't have to be complicated. I was making it that way. Jason was absolutely right about me not caring what people thought. *Ugh. But this is my job.*

He had done me a favor taking me on at the firm, but it was a favor I'd wanted since I was, like, fifteen. I'd already learned so much from him. That had always been my agenda. Work for Jason. Work with Jason. Learn from Jason. Possibly teach him a thing or two about the modern world and technology.

I grinned. I'd already gotten a bid on some new scanning software and a quote on a new email system to send password-protected emails to clients. It was secure, and it made sense in this day and age. As far as I was concerned, he was going to have to do it.

The door from the garage creaked above me. Footsteps thudded on the ceiling. Finally, my dad was home. I knew my dad. He needed time. Since I'd given him some space, we could have a reasonable conversation about my life.

I dressed quickly and ran a brush through my hair. When I ascended the stairs, my dad was sitting at the kitchen table in the dark. A half-full beer sat in front of him. My heart twisted. He looked like he'd aged overnight. I hadn't meant for it to be this way for him. I'd actually envisioned that he would be happy for us—thrilled I'd fallen in love with someone he could count on. If Dad could count on Jason, that meant Dad could count on him to keep his daughter safe. So much for wishful thinking.

"Dad?"

He stared out into the backyard, ignoring me.

I stepped into the kitchen, poured myself a beer with a little too much foam, and sat at the table across from him.

"Can we talk?" Even though I was full of confidence about this, I hated that my voice was shaky.

He turned to me. Anguish marred his features, and my heart dipped into my belly. "What do you want to talk about? I think we've gotten everything out in the air at this point."

"No, we haven't. I need you to trust me on this, Dad. I'm a good girl. A good daughter." I laid my hands on the table. "Falling in love with someone who is twice my age doesn't make me a bad person."

"I never said it did."

"That's how you're making it. Yes, it was a mistake to keep it from you. To hide it. But falling in love isn't a mistake. It doesn't matter who it's with." Love was love, and he knew that.

"I'm befuddled as to how something like this even started, Quinn. One of my best friends? Out of all the men in the world, why the hell are you doing prancing around with him?"

Telling him about my whole sexual journey seemed weird, but essential for him to understand. Did I tell him how this all started with the incident? I took a drink of my beer. "I don't know how much you want to hear, but I found myself attracted to him. Things progressed. Once I started working at the office, we realized there was a lot about one another that we liked. Enjoyed spending time together. All that kind of stuff."

"What happened to the Billy kid you brought around?"

"Dad. All the boys I've ever dated are just that. Boys. Jason has so much more to offer than Bill." I inhaled a deep breath then tried to explain. "Jason was something different. New. The way he moved. The way he spoke and acted. He was so much more mature and kinder. He wasn't full of drama or anything." I chuckled, thinking about me daring him to cover my mouth in his office earlier. "If anything, I'm the immature one in our relationship. But anyway, I want Jason. He wants me. He's helped me..." What kind of word did I use to explain to my dad that Jason had helped me broaden my sexuality? "Grow. He's helped me grow. A lot."

"This has totally blindsided me, Quinn."

"I know. I'm sorry. I really am. But this isn't about hurting you or surprising you. I'm not sorry I feel the way I do about him, though. Neither of us was expecting our relationship to turn into this."

"It was just going to be sex?" My dad slammed a hand on the table. "How could Jason do this to me?"

"He didn't do anything to you. Was he not forthcoming? Yes. Did he break some unknown bro code? Probably. But I'm an adult, and I think the bro code is overrated. Out of all the guys I've dated, Jason is the best, and if you weren't so angry right now, you would see how happy I am."

My dad took a long swallow of his beer, stood, and refilled it. He sat back down across from me, which was saying something. He wasn't so mad that he was walking out. "I'm beside myself. I don't know what to do."

"Dad, you don't have to do anything but accept this. Jason is a great guy. I've known it all my life. I've always loved him, but these past few months, I've seen a softer side of him. I've gotten to really know him. He's gotten to know me. We like what we've learned about one another. We enjoy each other. We enjoy working together."

"Our friends—they're going to think I'm crazy for allowing this to happen."

"First of all, it's none of their business. Second of all, you aren't *allowing* anything to happen or not happen because I'm a grownup. And third of all, according to Jason, all the guys your age would be thrilled to be dating a twenty-six-year-old like me." I gave him a big smile and shrugged. "Just saying."

"So what happens from here? Are you moving in together? Getting married?" He blinked. "Wow. I'd have to walk you down the aisle and then go stand in for the best man role."

I chuckled. My dad was coming around. "That would be so weird. But yeah, you probably would have to do that. At any rate, we haven't talked about marriage. We're enjoying one another for the time we have together." I stood, leaving my half-full beer on the table. "I promise that you will be the first to hear about any kind of wedding talk. If that were to ever happen."

My dad stood and let out a deep breath. "This is what I mean, Quinn. This is what worries me. The logical way is that two people fall madly in love and talk about a future together. Then they plan a wedding. Get married. Have kids. And here you are, placating the fact that you haven't talked about marriage. You've always wanted a big, beautiful wedding, kids—am I wrong? I think I at least know that about my daughter."

"You're not wrong."

"But see, because he's older, this hasn't come up, or you're accepting certain things. Have you talked about kids and how Jason would feel about that? He's raised two already. Is he really wanting to chase after toddlers at his age?"

The look on my face must have answered my dad's question.

He shook his head. "See? This is what worries me. He's older. He's had some of these things already. He doesn't want to start back over. He may not even want to get married again after Holly. Plus, you guys are on different levels of life. You're young and should be at karaoke night with Hannah every Wednesday night. Not sitting with Jason at home, wasting away such precious years. You only live once. You have to experience it all."

"It's been nine weeks, Dad." But he wasn't wrong. I couldn't deny what he was saying. Jason and I hadn't really talked about this kind of serious stuff. Between all the amazing sex, work, and both of us believing that this was for fun, the long-term never came up. "You're right about all of that. We're not that serious yet. Jason and I barely just discovered how deep our feelings for one another run. Can we enjoy that for five minutes? Before we start getting too deep into talking about marriage and babies."

My dad nodded.

"Plus, I'm barely starting my career. I can't have kids myself any time soon. So for me, that's off the table for a while now."

"Exactly. And let's pretend that you and Jason are in love, getting married, the full shebang. What if he wants kids now? Sooner rather than later? You know how hard kids are, let alone having one at fifty-three?"

"I hadn't thought about that."

"I bet not. But this is why you have such a smart dad. To make you think about these things." He gave me his first real smile.

"You're not mad at me anymore, are you?

"No. I'm not mad. I want you to be happy."

"You're not going to give Jason a bad time, are you? In all honesty, he wanted to tell you. I was the one who was afraid to."

"If you mean give Jason a bad time like I would to any of

my daughter's suitors, then yes. I'll be treating him the same. Only the best for you."

"Dad, don't. That would be so embarrassing."

My dad shrugged. "I have to vet all guys my daughter brings home."

I pulled him in for a tight hug. "Thanks for listening to me. I'm sorry we didn't tell you before." I pulled away. "Now, tell me about this woman you're seeing."

My dad shrugged sheepishly. "Her name is Lorainne. She's a nurse."

"Oh wow. At the hospital?"

He nodded. "Not in pediatrics. But we've been running into each other a lot, and she asked me out."

I swear my dad's ego went up a notch.

"Turns out your ol' dad still has some looks to him." He did a little jig—moving his shoulders forward and backward.

"Oh gosh. You're a dork. So what's she like?"

"She's nice. She's obviously nothing like your mom—"

"Obviously," I said.

"But she talks a lot and fills the silence. And I like it. Doesn't make me feel so lonely."

My heart wept at his words. "I get it. What else? She divorced? Have kids too? What?"

"She does have one son. He's eighteen, getting ready to graduate."

My dad glanced away and back to me. "Actually, she's a little younger than me."

The wrinkles in my forehead tightened. "How much younger?"

"Just ten years." He shrugged. "Not much. Not twenty."

For fuck's sake.

IT MADE me cringe to think about kids and marriage with anyone. My dad was right. I did want both. But I didn't know *when* I wanted them. Was it too soon to be in love with someone if I didn't know the answers to those questions, especially when I didn't know the answers for him either? I would have been shocked if Jason wanted more kids. Like my dad had said, why would he? He was at the point in his life where he could fly with the wind, having zero cares in the world. How important it was to me, though?

Marriage? Yes. I wanted that. I'd never planned on having kids the minute I got married; that was for sure. Being a lawyer meant I had to build a strong career first. Did I really, deep in my heart, want a child?

The idea made my stomach turn. I wasn't ready for a child—whether Jason was or wasn't.

I pulled into his driveway, automatically going to pull into his garage, but I stopped, realizing I no longer had to do that.

He came around the corner of the house, wearing denim shorts and carrying a rake. No shirt. His smile warmed me from the inside out. He leaned against my open door. "Hey." He leaned in and kissed me. "How did it go with Greg last night?"

"Better than I thought. He's all good now." I gave him a once-over. "You need help?" I glanced up at the sky. "Before it starts raining. I brought homemade lasagna."

"Yum." He gave me a wicked smile. "Come on. Just raking some dead grass and leaves. Cutting down a few random bushes that popped up." I followed him through his fence and into his backyard. "So, what did Greg say?"

"Umm. He said that I needed to examine the choices I'm making by being with you."

"Meaning?"

"Meaning that neither of us knows where we're going from here. We've never talked about a future together because we were so sure we weren't going to have one. But here we are." I gestured. "He brought up some valid points about being a man at your age, you probably wouldn't want kids. Maybe not even want to get married again."

Jason stopped walking, and I ran into him. "What do you want, Q? I meant what I said. I love you. If having a relationship with you means kids, then I would have five more. As far as marriage goes, you know I'll give you whatever you want as long as you're happy." He winced. "But..."

"But what?"

"Are we there yet?" Worry was etched into his forehead like he might be saying the wrong thing, and I busted up laughing.

"No. No, we're not. But it's still something we should at least know about one another."

He dropped the rake, and it landed on the grass with a small thunk. He pulled me into his arms. "Leave it to Greg to think of all the important shit."

"Well, he made valid points that I couldn't argue with. To put your mind at ease, I don't want kids now. Maybe never. Building my career is more important right now. But you have changed that for me. You've allowed me to see what I really want—not the expectation that I'm a woman I should have children—but that it's no one's choice but mine and the man I'm with. Obviously, you will be at an age where it would be hard to crawl on your knees chasing a toddler, and frankly, Counselor, I'm not sure I want that. Period."

Jason lifted me off the ground and swung me around. I giggled.

"But marriage. I do want that. But let's take this one day at a time. The biggest things happening in my life right now are giving you everything I can to make you happy, making sure Scanberg pays for his crimes, and making sure I pass the bar."

"You know what would really make me happy right now?"

With my arms wrapped around his neck, my feet still swinging in the air from him holding me up, I searched his face. "What would make you happy right now?"

"If you would move in with me."

20

JASON

"Move in with you? You don't think it's too soon?"

I set Quinn down and took one of the seats at my patio table. I patted my lap, indicating that she should sit. "No. You do?"

Great. I'd spoken too soon. It had been a whirlwind in some ways, but in other ways, it was as if we were destined for one another. I had to make things right with Greg. Then all would be good, assuming he didn't tell me to go to hell. If I had to make a choice between him being my friend and Quinn being my girlfriend, it would make for awkward Christmases and Thanksgivings.

"No. I guess not. I mean, I don't really at all. I don't want to make you think this is necessary or anything like that. I want you to be in this with me and not think you have to do anything because of my dad." She chewed on her bottom lip.

"You moving in with me has absolutely nothing to do with Greg. I'm asking because I want to see you all the time —as much as you'll put up with me. I want to cook dinner together every night instead of once or twice a week. Sleep in on the weekends. Wake up in the middle of the night and be able to reach for your naked body."

She gave me a sly grin. "Who says I sleep naked?"

"Me. That's who." I traced a hand over her cheek, along her neck, and down her chest. "But the truth is, it doesn't matter what you sleep in because I'll relish the joy of undressing you."

"Yes. Yes. Yes. Yes." She squeezed my neck. "As long as you're super sure."

I nibbled on her neck, inhaling her scent. "I'm super sure."

"Good. I've been practicing making homemade chai lattes, and I think you're going to fall in love with them. Can't wait for you to try one."

"Hmmm. I don't know. It'll be hard to beat the coffee shop by my office," he teased.

I feigned shock, and we both laughed. He got serious, rubbing a finger across my bottom lip. "They'll probably be the best I've ever had."

"But now about work."

"What about it?"

"We have to figure out how I'm going to establish my independence at the office. At least while I'm your clerk."

I squeezed one eye shut. "What do you mean?"

"Well, don't you think after the eight weeks I've worked for you I've established that I know what you expect of me? I do everything you need and sometimes—not always, but most of the time—I know what you need from me before you ask."

"I would have to agree with that."

"Good. Thank you." She shifted in my lap and gave me her most serious expression. "I would like to have your blessing to change the way you do things."

"Meaning?" I knew in my gut it was her whole technology spiel. But I wanted to give her the satisfaction.

"Meaning that we have to bring Richter, Richter & Salazar up-to-date with the modern age of technology. We have to start saving trees." She put her hand up. "And you could still use paper and your cute little file folders as you see fit, but for everyone and everything else, we need to scan the documents. We need to utilize a special e-mail system to stay in contact with clients that is password-protected for confidentiality. We need an electronic calendar shared between the two of us so I can see what appointments you have and when you'll be in court—it would save time from having to ask—and then—"

"Q, I think that all sounds like a great idea."

She opened her mouth like she was going to argue, and it must have dawned on her that I was in agreement with her. "What?"

"I agree. I think you're absolutely right about the updates. It's a way to bring Richter, Richter & Salazar into the digital age. Sounds great."

If I had my phone handy, I would have taken a picture of her, smiling and happy. She warmed my heart. "Wow. That wasn't as hard as I thought it was going to be."

"After you mentioned it the first time, I was swamped and really couldn't think about it. But I've had time to think about it, and I'm good with it. You're in charge of getting us all hooked up, though. I don't have the time, nor do I want to make the time. It's your baby."

"Deal. I've reached out to a few companies already, so I'm at a starting point." She put her arms around me and squeezed. "Thank you."

"You're welcome."

"Now. I might need your help with the Scanberg thing."

"How? You don't need my help. This is all you. How many girls have you spoken with?"

"Fifty? But only seven, so far, have agreed. But I know there are more than seven."

I nodded. "I would probably guess that too. The scary part is that he's probably been doing this his entire career." I didn't like the way that made me feel. If the guy weren't already dying a slow, miserable death, I would have liked to punch his fucking eyes out for treating young women that way.

"I made a friend in his old department, and she's been helping me research students that were in his class for the past seven years. And the department is run by different people. None of the ones that worked with Scanberg are even there anymore."

"So maybe they discovered this, and before it could get into a big scandal, the board of trustees fired everyone? Quietly cleaning house."

"Maybe." She shrugged. "Anyway, it's hard because some of these women have graduated and married so they don't have the same last name to look up on social media."

"Is that how you're finding people?" That was the most unorthodox thing I'd ever heard.

"Duh. Everyone has at least one social media account these days. That's how you find people in the normal world." Her forehead got all wrinkly. "You didn't think I was actually looking through a phone book, did you?"

"What if they aren't on social media? Then what's your plan?"

Quinn shrugged. "Background check? But everyone is on something."

"I'm not."

Quinn scrunched her nose at me. "You're an exception. I mean, how do you not even have a LinkedIn account?"

"Did you already look?" The thought that she was searching for me online pumped up my ego some.

"Ah, yeah. That first night I watched you getting head. I couldn't find anything. Oh, and that's another thing. A website. You don't even have a website. When I Googled your name, some random website came up listing your name and the number of years you've been in practice. It also listed that you graduated from Washburn's School of Law. So random."

"So you're saying Richter, Richter & Salazar needs a website?"

"Yes. Of course. It'll land you guys more business just by being there for someone to call."

Pride swelled in my chest for this woman. Thunder boomed in the distance, and rain started to pelt down on us. She tilted her head toward the sky and began to laugh while raindrops landed on her face. It took my breath away, watching her enjoying this and living in this moment, of allowing me to share a part of her life with her.

She glanced at me, and we shared a brief moment of contentedness before desire pulsed through her and into me. Then we were smashing our faces together, kissing one another for everything we were worth. My hand traveled down to her hips, and I shifted her so I could stand, and her legs were wrapped around my waist.

I laid her down on my chaise lounge chair and made quick work of peeling her sodden clothes off before they got to be too sticky. Her hands smoothed across my chest hair. Then she went to town on unbuttoning my shorts. The thunder growled and replicated the sounds of my heart as my cock sprang free.

Raindrops pelted her breasts and nipples. Her lips. Her tongue swiped her bottom lip, licking up the water. My heart had never craved someone so badly.

She tugged on my dick, moving from my head to the base of my cock in quick jerks. I pulled her up off the lounge chair and lay on my back. "Get on me and ride me with that pretty pussy."

She slid down balls deep onto my cock, positioning her feet so she was pitched above me, working herself up and down on me the way those fake horses move on a carousel pole. *Damn. My woman was learning new tricks.*

I could already feel the come starting to build, and I settled my hands on her hips to keep her from moving. "No more. I'm going to lose it."

"That's. What. I. Like." She bobbed up and down.

Two could play this game. I pressed my fingers into her clit, hoping this would be enough to make her lose control. Water dripped off the strands of her hair, flowing in perfect little streams across her tits. The pain of pleasure was so great that I couldn't make myself lean forward and lick the water droplets off her the way I would've liked.

"Jason," Quinn whimpered into the rainy sky, and she convulsed around me, dragging my own orgasm out.

"Quinn." The sky opened up and poured on us worse than it was. The ground was already covered in at least an inch of standing puddles. Thunder boomed. Lightning cracked across the sky.

"I love you," she yelled over the storm. "And I'm super excited that you love me back."

I laughed and hollered, "Let's go inside and finish what we started."

It wasn't until the next morning, after I'd made Quinn breakfast in bed, that the unfinished business I had forced me into a hot shower. I wrote Quinn a note that I'd gone to see her dad and left it on the pillow for her to find when she woke up.

I HESITATED when I stepped up to the front porch. Should I walk in like I had for the past twenty-five years? Or should I knock because now I was in a whole other level of friends? Some could almost argue we were strangers now because of the chances that they hadn't seen Quinn and my relationship coming.

Fuck.

I went to press the doorbell then stopped. I was being a fool. *What the fuck is wrong with me?* I was acting like I didn't know the first thing about being in love.

I pulled open the screen door and stepped inside. I glanced at the family picture of Greg, Debra, Quinn, and Elizabeth. *We've come a long way, Brenning family.*

The music was on low, and Greg was sitting at the kitchen table, going through his mail. He raised an eyebrow when I stepped into the living room. "Make yourself at home."

"It seemed too strange to knock. Even if you are pissed at me." I took the seat across from him.

"Where's Quinn? At your place, I'm assuming. She didn't come home last night."

"Yes, she's safe and sound. You know that, right? I'll always keep her safe."

"You always have."

I shut my eyes then opened them. "Then can we go back to normal? I'm in love with Quinn. I didn't intend it to happen that way. But I'm still the same guy. I'm a good man. I'm always going to treat Quinn—and you—with the utmost respect."

"Really? I don't feel respected. I feel betrayed. She's young. Rebellious. Impulsive. But you"—he pointed a finger at me—"are a grown man. Seasoned. You should have known better." He closed his eyes briefly. "Can you for one second put yourself in my shoes? Imagine walking into my office and finding me fucking your daughter."

I looked away, sharing the pain of a father at having to see something like that. "I can't."

"Exactly. It's a hard fucking pill to swallow. So excuse me if on day two, I'm still upset with you."

"I get it. As long as you know that you know me, and I think you also know that I will treat Quinn right and respect her. Give her whatever it is she needs to succeed. Love her. Trust her. Stand by her side." I cleared my throat when Greg gave me a strange look. "As long as she'll have me."

"You really love her." He said it almost reluctantly.

"Thank you. Look, we may think I'm the wrong guy for her—at least I did think that until I realized she brings out the best of me—but the important thing is that Quinn believes I'm the right guy for her." I placed my palms flat on the table. "You have my word that I will be the guy she believes I am."

Greg stared at me for a long time. I wasn't going to cower. I meant what I'd said. I prayed like hell that he would get over this because in the end, we'd been through a fucking lot together. I wanted to continue living our lives still going through shit together.

It felt like five minutes went by.

"You better not break her heart. And know that she is young, could want a family and marriage in the future."

"I got it. And honestly, whatever Quinn wants, I'll give it to her. I'm okay getting married again. I have a clearer mind on the things I want in life. What makes me happy. I'm not someone who would say no to marriage again just because the first one didn't end well."

Greg nodded. Then he walked to the counter, got out two glasses, and filled them with beer. He turned to me. "Never too early to share a much-needed drink between friends."

I stood and took the glass he offered. "You are right about that."

Clink.

21

QUINN

"Thank God the DA's office indicted him. I couldn't have done this without your help." Jason and I were sitting inside the coffee shop a few blocks from the office. It had become our routine on mornings we didn't have court, and it was the best part of my day, aside from when we made dinner together. But in the mornings, out like this, I felt the most blessed to have him in my life.

He was having his standard chai latte, and I was enjoying a maple latte with an extra shot of espresso because ever since I moved in with him, our sleeping hours were spent on each other. Sleep seemed to be an afterthought. He smiled at me over his drink. The sun was shining brightly, making all the gray strands in his hair sparkle. He looked amazing. As usual.

"You could have done it without my help. Besides, I didn't help much. This time, you did all the work, and I was merely your assistant."

"You can be my assistant anytime. Scanberg tried to play up the cancer card when they arrested him. Claimed he was too sick to go to jail."

Jason waved a hand like he was shooing a fly away. "They give him whatever he needs medically. They can't deny him that."

"Do you think he'll be able to post bond?"

Jason shook his head. "Probably. He's got the assets to. When is his arraignment?"

"Thursday." I blinked away the tears that started to well up in my eyes. "I keep getting texts from a few of the girls thanking me for taking this on. For wanting justice. For standing up for them when they couldn't."

"Well, it's a big deal. Some of those girls had to seek therapy for the things he did." Jason shook his head. "I can't believe the woman with the video didn't go to authorities anyway."

I shrugged. "The good thing is that she is now, and she has a great group of women that have her back. One of the women, Lee, started a non-profit organization for women who have been sexually assaulted. It's amazing how much impact he had on these women. It wasn't like he raped them, but he took away their confidence. Their sense of security. Their unconditional trust in people."

"Have I told you lately how proud I am of you? That your future will continue to be amazing because you're intelligent, resilient, beautiful, and confident."

My heart tripled in size, and I ducked my head. He has told me these things, but every time he said them, it made me blush. "You have. I'm learning from the best." Smirking, I raised my coffee cup, and he nudged it with his.

"To the amazing law career that awaits you."

"You're silly. Thank you." I glanced at my phone. "I have to go. I have a client meeting me at the office in twenty minutes."

"I figure that's enough time to sneak into the bathroom here and have my way with you."

I laughed. "We can't do that."

I looked around the coffee shop. Three baristas were making coffees for the drive-through, and a few people sat around reading the paper and working away on their computers.

"I'm going to use the restroom." Grabbing my bag, I stood then leaned across the table. "I may or may not be wearing panties under this dress."

I smiled when I heard his chair scoot across the floor, and the thud of his footsteps followed me down the hallway. It was fun being naughty.

EPILOGUE

I fidgeted on my stool and kept my nose down, looking at my cucumber martini. I didn't do the bar scene that much anymore. My blood boiled at the thought of all of my hard work and not being able to ever have a chance of giving all of those women hope that Scanberg would rot in jail and pay for his crimes. Cassie. Kayla. Chrissy. Tamara. They all had names to me and had been just another female body to Scanberg.

At least he'd been formally arraigned and charged for his crimes before his death. The women would at least have that—and, of course, the security that he would never hurt another woman again, may he rest in hell.

He's dead, Quinn.

I had learned that the university had cleaned house and quietly gotten rid of the person who'd hid Kayla's complaint and threatened her scholarship. That person had also passed away seven months ago in a jet-skiing accident. That was still a hard pill to swallow.

Now, my biggest case was for a credit union that had decided to bypass the rules and regulations of a few large commercial loans, and I was in the process of doing depositions.

"This seat taken?"

I glanced up from my drink, trying not to chuckle and play this right. "No. You can sit here."

Jason sat down next to me. He waved the bartender over. "Bourbon, please." He turned to me, his eyes glistening. "You want another drink?"

"I'm good. This is my second one." I smoothed the wrinkles in my skirt. "What's your name?"

"Jason. And you are?"

"Quinn. My name is Quinn."

Jason took his drink from the bartender and took a long swallow, practically downing the entire drink. "Great name for a beautiful woman." He winked at me. "I love the color purple, by the way."

I couldn't help but laugh. I glanced down at my blouse. It was the deep purple like our blindfold, his tie, and my ribbon lingerie that I still wore for him—his favorite color. Was it silly we were playing this game? Kind of. But it was fun. New. Different. "Are you here alone?"

He nodded and took another sip.

I leaned forward in my seat. "I have a secret. If I tell you, do you promise not to talk too loudly about it?"

Jason's eyebrows rose high. "You have my word."

I rested my hand on his forearm and leaned in even closer. This was my man. He smelled good, like bourbon, sandalwood cologne, and our laundry soap that somehow always smelled better on him than me. I pressed my lips to the curve of his ear. "I have a toy stuck in my ass right now."

He pulled back and looked at me in shock, arousal, need. "Are you being serious?"

I laughed again. "As serious as I am on a court day. I have a room upstairs. Care to join me?"

He swallowed the rest of his drink and reached into the front pocket of his jeans for cash to pay. The outline of his cock pressed against the fabric, and I clenched my thighs together. He was solid. Big. Ready. It had been a chore to get the lubrication and do it to myself before we drove over here, but I'd done it. I had the bottle in my purse. I wanted this. I wanted to give it to him. I wanted him to have my virginity this way. Only him. Always him. Forever him.

"Let's go."

He held out his hand. I stuck my hand in his, and he all but ran out of the bar and across the lobby to the bank of elevators. He pressed the button and turned to me. "I'm so lucky to have you."

I shook my head. "I'm lucky to have you."

The doors slid open, and he tugged me inside and up against the back wall, where he devoured my lips with his. Possessive and greedy. Demanding. He bit my lips. His hand found its way between my legs and panties to my wet entrance. His fingers slid into my pussy while the elevator took us up, aiding us on this high.

Ding.

Jason pulled away. His eyes were lidded. Hungry for me. My pussy throbbed and ached for him. My heart was full. I laughed as we ran down the hall and scanned our key card, gaining access to our room.

"Surprise," Jason said softly behind me.

The room was extravagant. Rose petals were strewn all over the room—on the floor, the bed, and the nightstands. In the corner of the room, a bank of steps led to an oversized bathtub. I gasped. "This is beautiful."

He undressed me slowly, kissing and licking every inch

of my skin that he exposed. I swallowed. "Tonight is supposed to be all about you."

He was already shaking his head. "No, Q. It's about us. And right now, I want you to come all over my mouth."

He pushed my legs apart, then his greedy mouth was all over me. It was as if every time we were together, it was new. The joy and pleasure that coursed through my veins—all of it was newer, fresher, and more exciting than the last time we'd made love. Over and over, we brought each other to new heights. My orgasm pulsed on the brink. His fingers dipped inside me, and I was done. My clit quivered with wave after wave of pleasure.

"How do you manage to do that every time?" I breathed.

"Do what?"

"Make it better than the last time?"

A deep chuckle rose from his throat. "It's the company, I guess."

I pointed to my purse, and he opened it then pulled out the bottle of lubricant. "I want to undress you and put my lips on you first, and then we are doing this."

"You're not going to get any arguments from me."

I stood and unbuckled his slacks, pulling them off his legs. I pulled his boxer briefs down, loving the way his cock sprang out, standing so tall and proud like a flagpole. I crawled onto the bed. "It isn't bothering you stuck in there?"

The anal plug.

"No. It's in, it's in. It's fine. It's been almost an hour, so it's practically a part of me at this point." I laughed. "Just teasing. But seriously, it's okay."

I got on my knees and leaned over him, taking his dick into my mouth, swallowing him as far as I could. I wanted this night to be perfect for him. He was always so kind and caring for me. I wanted to do the same for him. I wanted to give him his ultimate fantasy.

He only let me do it for a few minutes before he pulled me to my feet and made me get on all fours on the bed. He circled my ass with his finger, pressing gently against my opening. The bottle of lubricant clicked open, then he was back at it, rubbing slickness around my opening. "Pull it out. Slow. Gently." I had researched this better than I'd ever thought I would. The key was lube. "Now, play with me."

He chuckled. It was cute. He was nervous.

"Don't be shy, stranger." I went back to our little game. "It's not every day you meet a woman that wants to give you your deepest desires."

"Damn straight it isn't." He slipped a finger in me, replacing the toy, and I clenched around him at the intrusion. "You okay?" he asked.

"Yes." It was... different. Not really painful now that I'd used that toy. It wasn't unbearable. But how the hell was his cock going to fit in there? "No way you're going to fit in there."

"I'll fit." He sounded amused. "I'm not *that* big."

I snorted. "Going the modest route, I see." Thankfully, I'd prepped some. I wanted to give him something he'd fantasized about for so long.

His other hand rubbed my clit, flicking the sensitive skin back and forth. His lips pressed down against the curve of one of my butt cheeks. "I'm never going to get enough of you."

He slid his fingers inside my pussy, and I rocked against him. This was not enough. My ass stretched a bit farther when he inserted a second finger. I sucked in a breath. Again, not unbearable, just different. And still, not enough. While he had both hands full, I began to rub my clit. It was obscene, almost shameful what he was doing to me, but I was loving every minute of it.

"That's my girl. Come for me."

He always knew when I was close. His low voice always put me over the edge. He moved in and out of me quicker, and I rubbed faster. In seconds, I was turning into jelly. He slowly removed his fingers, and I definitely felt the loss on my backside.

"I'll be right back."

I heard the water running in his bathroom, then he was back. "You still want this?" He was naked, holding the bottle of lube in his hands and a condom in the other. He held up the condom. "For easy cleanup."

I nodded.

The lube was slick against my skin and the motions of him rubbing it across my crease made me feel every bit as sexy as he always made me feel. The condom wrapper crinkled in the quiet, then the head of his cock pressed into my entrance.

I tensed.

Deep breath. Relax. I pushed my muscles out, and Jason slipped in. Instantly, I was hit with a burning sensation along the rim. I gritted my teeth. I clenched my eyes shut, and he was kind enough to hold still while I adjusted to his girth in the foreign place, which was practically forgotten while I teased my throbbing, aching clit.

"Tell me if you change your mind."

Jason inched into me slowly until he was flush against my ass. It wasn't anything like the nightmarish sexual fantasy I'd imagined. It didn't hurt. It was just... there, pressing into me, turning me on more than I already was because it was such a foreign place for him to be and not at all as crazy as I'd built up in my mind. My clit throbbed with each pass of my fingers, and Jason's thrusts into my ass went deeper still.

"I'm dying." His voice was gruff, and he started pushing in and out of me, fucking my ass like we'd always talked about. "I'm not going to last long like this."

I couldn't help my smile. That was one of the many things I loved about him. His honesty. And the way I could make him powerless. I was full of him.

Then Jason's hand was there against my clit, sticking his fingers inside me, filling both holes. I pressed against his palm, riding his hand while he fucked my ass. We came together in a mass of groans and heavy breathing, then he was slipping out of me. I knew I would let him do that again if he ever wanted. Anything to make him happy. He pulled me to my feet.

"You okay?" he asked again.

"I'm good. It wasn't like I imagined. I guess the key is lube and stretching, huh?"

His dimples came out. "I think you're right. Come on. Shower first, then the tub?"

I nodded. I followed him to the bathroom where he disposed of the condom and turned on the shower.

"I may have even stocked the room with bourbon and a cigar for us to enjoy because I don't have any plans on sleeping tonight." He playfully smacked my ass. "And I hope you don't either."

"You sure you'll be able to hack an all-nighter? Plus, we can't smoke in a hotel room. We'll have to wait until we get home."

"Baby, I got us covered." He stepped in the shower stream and pulled me in with him. "This isn't a smoke-free room, so we're good."

He took the bar of soap and rubbed it across my tits. He looked into my eyes, and my heart increased in tempo.

"Thank you for that, Q."

"Your wish is my command, Counselor."

Five Billionaires who enjoy their bachelor status.
Five women who bring them to their knees.

Read on for a peek of LUCKY RIDE, an Irresistible Billionaires prequel.

Chapter One

KADE THREADED a hand through his hair, standing alongside the interstate on-ramp. His jaw ached, and he made a point to try to stop grinding his teeth. He was supposed to be in Vegas yesterday for Alex's wedding, but work had prevented him from leaving. Naturally. And now they had not one but two flat tires before they even got on the interstate. His driver paced the edge of the on-ramp back and forth, yakking into his phone. The cold air blew off the mountains, threatening snow. Kade's plane was scheduled to leave in two hours. How in the hell was he going to get to Denver International Airport in time, even if Roger got another vehicle?

Cars whirred past the two of them, and Kade stepped

back to protect his suit from the gravel kicked up by other cars. "Why today?" he yelled into the air.

The jarring sound of gravel crunching behind him pulled his attention. A dark-blue sedan that had seen better days slowed to a stop behind their vehicle. Great. It was likely someone thinking they could be of assistance. The tinted windows made it impossible for him to see inside, and unless they gave him their car, they would be zero help. *Nice try.*

Once all the vehicles passed, the car door opened, and a dirty white tennis shoe hit the ground. He came face to face with *her.*

Eden Wilcox.

Even though it had been four years, he would recognize her anywhere. He distinctly remembered what she was wearing the last time he saw her. Who would have thought she would be coming to his rescue?

Her brown hair was longer than he remembered, trailing down to the middle of her back, a whisper above her ass, in waves that would make the ocean jealous. She had grown curves in all the right places, sending heat straight to his dick. Even in baggy sweatpants, she was still very beautiful. Still very annoying. A pair of black sunglasses were propped on top of her head, allowing him the opportunity to really see her. The wide grin she tossed at him stole his breath.

I don't like this. Like I'm a damsel in distress.

He held in a groan. *Oh, but aren't I?*

"Fancy seeing you here." She winked.

Eden stepped over the white line briefly before moving around her car, coming to a stop in front of him. Her feminine, floral smell wafted his way, and he hated that it made him immediately think of her lying spread-eagle on his bed.

"I need a ride."

She raised a disapproving brow at him, clearly enjoying his situation. "Obviously. Looks like today is your lucky day."

He grimaced. "Define lucky."

"I'm here, aren't I?"

"I see you're still feisty as hell."

Alex's little sister gave him a tight smile. "I see you're still an asshole. I *thought* I would be nice and offer you a ride. But"—she put a hand on her hip and shrugged—"changed my mind." She turned back toward her car.

Kade laid a hand on her shoulder, desperation winning out. "I do need a ride. I assume you're on your way to your brother's wedding?"

"Wow, genius. How long did it take you to figure that out?"

"Can I go with you?"

Eden pulled her sunglasses off her head, and her gaze hit him square in the gut. Damn it, why was she so beautiful? Why did he have to notice? She pursed her lips like she was holding a secret from him. "Is my car good enough for you? Not worried about your suit getting too dirty, are you?"

Kade looked down at the crisp gray lines of his suit and stark-blue tie. "I can always buy another one if your car ruins this one."

She scoffed. "Wow. Throwing away money like it's trash." Eden tilted her head toward Roger. "Does he need a ride too?"

"No. He'll wait with the car for a tow truck and a ride. Let me tell him I'm going with you and grab my suitcase."

Of course it would have to be his best friend's sister rescuing him. Why, God, why her? Roger covered the mouthpiece with his hand when Kade approached him.

Kade pointed to Eden. "She said she'll give me a ride to the airport. Text me once you have this figured out."

"Will do, boss. Sorry about this. Really sorry."

"Not your fault. Two flat tires seem deliberate."

"It sure does."

Kade turned and blew out a deep breath, steeling himself for the forty-minute ride to the airport with Eden. He pulled his suitcase out of his trunk, and the lid of her trunk popped open when he approached her car. If Kade could handle anything, it was a short ride with her. He could deal with her at the wedding. It wasn't like he would have to see her constantly while in Vegas, and that made the idea of pulling open her passenger-side door and sliding into her car that much more bearable. As did the sweet promise of first class on the plane.

"Buckle up." She put the car in drive, and he held up his hands in annoyance.

"You don't have to tell me to 'buckle up.' I know how riding in the passenger seat works."

"Do you?" She pursed her lips as she pulled onto the on-ramp and made her way to the interstate. "I wasn't sure if you always sat in the back seat being chauffeured around. Didn't know if the same rules applied."

Kade snorted. Maybe he couldn't handle the next forty minutes after all. "I am intelligent. A lot of people would actually tell you I'm one of the smartest people they know."

"What kind of people would that be? Your parents?" She stepped on the gas and switched lanes. She glanced at him with a raised brow. "Your harem?"

"My harem?"

"Of women. You can't deny you've been in the public spotlight. *Always* with different women."

"I can't help that there's plenty of me to go around."

Something flip-flopped in his chest. Before he could question what that specific feeling was, he tamped it down. "Keeping tabs on me, Eden?"

DOWNLOAD this brother's best friend romance when you join my newsletter!

www.subscribepage.com/ashleybostock

ALL THE THINGS

ALSO BY ASHLEY BOSTOCK

Irresistible Billionaires

Lucky Ride - a prequel

Nothing But Trouble

All Shook Up

No Strings Attached - a novella

Work For It

Feels Like Love - a novella

Love By Design

Now or Never - a novella

Playing For Keeps

Love in Lone Star

Wet

Wild

Wicked

Quickie Reads

Naughty Neighbor Series

Sex on Fire

Doggy Style

Sexting Virgin

Love Online Series

Text Activity

Text Appeal

Text You Up

Standalone Quickies

Mr. July

All I Want For Christmas

One Summer Night

ABOUT THE AUTHOR

Ashley Bostock was born and raised in Colorado, but her husband moved mountains to get her to Nebraska where they currently reside with their two children and her animals.
She stays busy daydreaming about the hot men she writes about in her novels.

She has traveled all over the world, but still has an extensive list of places she would love to visit. Anywhere near a sky-blue ocean will always be at the top of that list, although going back to South Africa's Kruger National Park to view the wildlife is a close second.

She carries a bachelor's degree in History with a concentration in Elementary Education from Metropolitan State College of Denver.
She has published over 18 books and is a USA Today bestselling author.

To Connect With Ashley
www.ashleybostock.com
ashley@ashleybostock.com

instagram.com/ashleybostock

facebook.com/authorashleybostock

tiktok.com/@ashley_bostock

bookbub.com/authors/ashley-bostock

goodreads.com/ashleybostock